A
TOR
DOUBLE
ACTION
WESTERN

Look for Tor Double Action Westerns from these authors

MAX BRAND
ZANE GREY
LEWIS B. PATTEN
WAYNE D. OVERHOLSER
CLAY FISHER
FRANK BONHAM
OWEN WISTER
STEVE FRAZEE*
HARRY SINCLAIR DRAGO*
JOHN PRESCOTT*
WILL HENRY*

*Coming soon

Zane Grey

PROSPECTOR'S GOLD
CANYON WALLS

TOR®

A TOM DOHERTY ASSOCIATES BOOK
NEW YORK

PROSPECTOR'S GOLD

CANYON WALLS

A Tor Book
Published by Tom Doherty Associates, Inc.
49 West 24th Street
New York, N.Y. 10010

Cover art by Bernal

ISBN: 0-812-50536-8

First Tor edition: August 1990

Printed in the United States of America

0 9 8 7 6 5 4 3 2 1

PROSPECTOR'S GOLD

1

TAPPAN GAZED DOWN UPON THE NEWLY-BORN LIT-
tle burro with something of pity and con-
sternation. It was not a vigorous offspring of
the redoubtable Jennie, champion of all the
numberless burros he had driven in his
desert-prospecting years. He could not leave
it there to die. Surely it was not strong
enough to follow its mother. And to kill it
was beyond him.

"Poor little devil!" soliloquized Tappan.
"Reckon neither Jennie nor I wanted it to be
born. . . . I'll have to hold up in this camp a
few days. You can never tell what a burro
will do. It might fool us an' grow strong all
of a sudden."

Whereupon Tappan left Jennie and her

tiny, gray lop-eared baby to themselves, and leisurely set about making permanent camp. The water at this oasis was not much to his liking, but it was drinkable, and he felt he must put up with it. For the rest the oasis was desirable enough as a camping site. Desert wanderers like Tappan favored the lonely water holes. This one was up under the bold brow of the Chocolate Mountains, where rocky wall met the desert sand, and a green patch of *palo verdes* and mesquites proved the presence of water. It had a magnificent view down a many-leagued slope of desert growths, across the dark belt of green and the shining strip of red that marked the Rio Colorado, and on to the upflung Arizona land, range lifting to range until the saw-toothed peaks notched the blue sky.

Locked in the iron fastnesses of these desert mountains was gold. Tappan, if he had any calling, was a prospector. But the lure of gold did not bind him to this wandering life any more than the freedom of it. He had never made a rich strike. About the best he could ever do was to dig enough gold to grubstake himself for another prospecting trip into some remote corner of the American Desert. Tappan knew the arid Southwest from San Diego to the Pecos River and from Picacho on the Colorado to the Tonto Basin. Few prospectors had the strength and endurance of Tappan. He was a giant in build, and at thirty-five had never yet reached the limit of his physical force.

With hammer and pick and magnifying glass Tappan scaled the bare ridges. He was not an expert in testing minerals. He knew he might easily pass by a rich vein of ore. But he did his best, sure at least that no prospector could get more than he out of the pursuit of gold. Tappan was more of a naturalist than a prospector, and more of a dreamer than either. Many were the idle moments that he sat staring down the vast reaches of the valleys, or watching some creature of the wasteland, or marveling at the vivid hues of desert flowers.

Tappan waited two weeks at this oasis for Jennie's baby burro to grow strong enough to walk. And the very day that Tappan decided to break camp he found signs of gold at the head of a wash above the oasis. Quite by chance, as he was looking for his burros, he struck his pick into a place no different from a thousand others there, and hit into a pocket of gold. He cleaned out the pocket before sunset, the richer for several thousand dollars.

"You brought me luck," said Tappan, to the little gray burro staggering round its mother. "Your name is Jenet. You're Tappan's burro, an' I reckon he'll stick to you."

Jenet belied the promise of her birth. Like a weed in fertile ground she grew. Winter and summer Tappan patrolled the sand beats from one trading post to another, and his burros traveled with him. Jenet had an especially good training. Her mother had happened to be a remarkably good burro before Tappan had bought her. And Tappan had patience; he found leisure to do things, and he had something of pride in Jenet. Whenever he happened to drop into Ehrenberg or Yuma, or any freighting station, some prospector always tried to buy Jenet. She grew as large as a medium-sized mule, and a three-hundred-pound pack was no load to discommode her.

Tappan, in common with most lonely wanderers of the desert, talked to his burro. As the years passed this habit grew, until Tappan would talk to Jenet just to hear the sound of his voice. Perhaps that was all which kept him human.

"Jenet, you're worthy of a happier life," Tappan would say, as he unpacked her after a long day's march over the barren land. "You're a ship of the desert. Here we are, with grub an' water, a hundred miles from any camp. An' what but you could have fetched me here? No horse! No mule! No man! Nothin' but a camel, an' so I call you ship of the desert. But for you an' your kind, Jenet, there'd be no prospectors, and few gold mines. Reckon the desert would be still an unknown waste. . . . You're a great beast

6

of burden, Jenet, an' there's no one to sing your praise."

And of a golden sunrise, when Jenet was packed and ready to face the cool, sweet fragrance of the desert, Tappan was wont to say:

"Go along with you, Jenet. The mornin's fine. Look at the mountains yonder callin' us. It's only a step down there. All purple an' violet! It's the life for us, my burro, an' Tappan's as rich as if all these sands were pearls."

But sometimes, at sunset, when the way had been long and hot and rough, Tappan would bend his shaggy head over Jenet, and talk in different mood.

"Another day gone, Jenet, another journey ended—an' Tappan is only older, wearier, sicker. There's no reward for your faithfulness. I'm only a desert rat, livin' from hole to hole. No home! No face to see. . . . Some sunset, Jenet, we'll reach the end of the trail. An' Tappan's bones will bleach in the sands. An' no one will know or care!"

When Jenet was two years old she would have taken the blue ribbon in competition with all the burros of the Southwest. She was unusually large and strong, perfectly proportioned, sound in every particular, and practically tireless. But these were not the only characteristics that made prospectors envious of Tappan. Jenet had the common virtues of all good burros magnified to an unbelievable degree. Moreover, she had sense and instinct that to Tappan bordered on the supernatural.

During these years Tappan's trail criss-crossed the mineral region of the Southwest. But, as always, the rich strike held aloof. It was like the pot of gold buried at the foot of the rainbow. Jenet knew the trails and the water holes better than Tappan. She could follow a trail obliterated by drifting sand or cut out by running water. She could scent at long distance a new spring on the desert or a strange water hole. She never wandered far from camp so that Tappan had to walk far in search of her. Wild burros, the bane of most prospectors, held no charm for Jenet. And she had never yet shown any especial liking for a tame burro. This was the strangest feature of Jenet's complex character. Burros were noted for their habit of pairing off, and forming friendships for one or more comrades. These relations were permanent. But Jenet still remained fancy free.

Tappan scarcely realized how he relied upon this big, gray, serene beast of burden. Of course, when chance threw him among men of his calling he would brag about her. But he had never really appreciated Jenet. In his way Tappan was a brooding, plodding fellow, not conscious of sentiment. When he bragged about Jenet it was her good qualities upon which he dilated. But what he really liked best about her were the little things of every day.

During the earlier years of her training Jenet had been a thief. She would pretend to be asleep for hours just to get a chance to steal something out of camp. Tappan had broken this habit in its incipiency. But he never quite trusted her. Jenet was a burro.

Jenet ate anything offered her. She could fare for herself or go without. Whatever Tappan had left from his own meals was certain to be rich dessert for Jenet. Every meal time she would stand near the camp fire, with one great long ear drooping, and the other standing erect. Her expression was one of meekness, of unending patience. She would lick a tin can until it shone resplendent. On long, hard, barren trails Jenet's deportment did not vary from that where the water holes and grassy patches were many. She did not need to have grass or grain. Brittle-bush and sage were good fare for her. She could eat greasewood, a desert plant that protected itself with a sap as sticky as varnish and far more dangerous to animals. She could eat cacti. Tappan had seen her break off leaves of the prickly pear cactus, and stamp upon them with her forefeet, mashing off the thorns, so that she could consume the succulent pulp. She liked mesquite beans, and leaves of willow, and all the trailing vines of the desert. And she could subsist in an arid waste land where a man would have died in short order.

No ascent or descent was too hard or dangerous for Jenet, provided it was possible of accomplishment. She would refuse a trail that was impassable. She seemed to have an uncanny instinct both for what she could do, and what was beyond a burro. Tappan had never known her to fail on something to which she stuck persistently. Swift streams of water, always bugbears for burros, did not stop Jenet. She hated quicksand, but could be trusted to navigate it, if that were possible. When she stepped gingerly, with little inch steps, out upon thin crust of ice or salty crust of desert sink hole, Tappan would know that it was safe, or she would turn back. Thunder and lightning, intense heat or bitter cold, the sirocco sand storm of the desert, the white dust of the alkali wastes— these were all the same to Jenet.

One August, the hottest and driest of his desert experience, Tappan found himself working a most promising claim in the lower reaches of the Panamint Mountains on the northern slope above Death Valley. It was a hard country at the most favorable season; in August it was terrible.

The Panamints were infested by various small gangs of desperadoes—outlaw claim jumpers where opportunity afforded—and out-and-out robbers, even murderers where they could not get the gold any other way.

Tappan had been warned not to go into

this region alone. But he never heeded any warnings. And the idea that he would ever strike a claim or dig enough gold to make himself an attractive target for outlaws seemed preposterous and not worth considering. Tappan had become a wanderer now from the unbreakable habit of it. Much to his amaze he struck a rich ledge of free gold in a canyon of the Panamints; and he worked from daylight until dark. He forgot about the claim jumpers, until one day he saw Jenet's long ears go up in the manner habitual with her when she saw strange men. Tappan watched the rest of that day, but did not catch a glimpse of any living thing. It was a desolate place, shut in, red-walled, hazy with heat, and brooding with an eternal silence.

Not long after that Tappan discovered boot tracks of several men adjacent to his camp and in an out-of-the-way spot, which persuaded him that he was being watched. Claim jumpers who were not going to jump his claim in this torrid heat, but meant to let him dig the gold and then kill him. Tappan was not the kind of man to be afraid. He grew wrathful and stubborn. He had six small canvas bags of gold and did not mean to lose them. Still, he was worried.

"Now, what's best to do?" he pondered. "I mustn't give it away that I'm wise. Reckon I'd better act natural. But I can't stay here longer. My claim's about worked out. An' these jumpers are smart enough to know it. . . . I've got to make a break at night. What to do?"

Tappan did not want to cache the gold, for in that case, of course, he would have to return for it. Still, he reluctantly admitted to himself that this was the best way to save it. Probably these robbers were watching him day and night. It would be most unwise to attempt escaping by traveling up over the Panamints.

"Reckon my only chance is goin' down into Death Valley," soliloquized Tappan, grimly.

The alternative thus presented was not to his liking. Crossing Death Valley at this season was always perilous, and never attempted in the heat of day. And at this particular time of intense torridity, when the day heat was unendurable and the midnight furnace gales were blowing, it was an enterprise from which even Tappan shrank. Added to this were the facts that he was too far west of the narrow part of the valley, and even if he did get across he would find himself in the most forbidding and desolate region of the Funeral Mountains.

Thus thinking and planning, Tappan went about his mining and camp tasks, trying his best to act natural. But he did not succeed. It was impossible, while expecting a shot at any moment, to act as if there was nothing on his mind. His camp lay at the bottom of a rocky slope. A tiny spring of water made verdure of grass and mesquite, welcome green in all that stark iron nakedness. His camp site was out in the open, on the bench near the spring. The gold claim that Tappan was working was not visible from any vantage point either below or above. It lay back at the head of a break in the rocky wall. It had two virtues—one that the sun never got to it, and the other that it was well hidden. Once there, Tappan knew he could not be seen. This, however, did not diminish his growing uneasiness. The solemn stillness was a menace. The heat of the day appeared to be augmenting to a degree beyond his experience. Every few moments Tappan would slip back through a narrow defile in the rocks and peep from his covert down at the camp. On the last of these occasions he saw Jenet out in the open. She stood motionless. Her long ears were erect. In an instant Tappan became strung with thrilling excitement. His keen eyes searched every approach to his camp. And at last in the gully below to the right he discovered two men crawling along from rock to rock. Jenet had seen them enter that gully and was now watching for them to appear.

Tappan's excitement gave place to a grimmer emotion. These stealthy visitors were going to hide in ambush, and kill him as he returned to camp.

"Jenet, reckon what I owe you is a whole lot," muttered Tappan. "They'd have got me sure. . . . But now—"

Tappan left his tools, and crawled out of his covert into the jumble of huge rocks toward the left of the slope. He had a six-shooter. His rifle he had left in camp. Tappan had seen only two men, but he knew there were more than that, if not actually near at hand at the moment, then surely not far away. And his chance was to worm his way like an Indian down to camp. With the rifle in his possession he would make short work of the present difficulty.

"Lucky Jenet's right in camp!" said Tappan, to himself. "It beats hell how she does things!"

Tappan was already deciding to pack and hurry away. On the moment Death Valley did not daunt him. This matter of crawling and gliding along was work unsuited to his great stature. He was too big to hide behind a little shrub or a rock. And he was not used to stepping lightly. His hobnailed boots could not be placed noiselessly upon the stones. Moreover, he could not progress without displacing little bits of weathered rock. He was sure that keen ears not too far distant could have heard him. But he kept on, making good progress around that slope to the far side of the canyon. Fortunately, he headed the gully up which his ambushers were stealing. On the other hand, this far side of the canyon afforded but little cover. The sun had gone down back of the huge red mass of the mountain. It had left the rocks so hot Tappan could not touch them with his bare hands.

He was about to stride out from his last covert and make a run for it down the rest of the slope, when, surveying the whole amphitheater below him, he espied the two men coming up out of the gully, headed toward his camp. They looked in his direction. Surely they had heard or seen him. But Tappan perceived at a glance that he was the closer to the camp. Without another moment of hesitation, he plunged from his hiding place, down the weathered slope. His giant strides set the loose rocks sliding and rattling. The men saw him. The foremost yelled to the one behind him. Then they both broke into a run. Tappan reached the level of the bench, and saw he could beat either of them into the camp. Unless he were disabled! He felt the wind of a heavy bullet before he heard it strike the rocks beyond. Then followed the boom of a Colt. One of his enemies had halted to shoot. This spurred Tappan to tremendous exertion. He flew over the rough ground, scarcely hearing the rapid shots. He could no longer see the man who was firing. But the first one was in plain sight, running hard, not yet seeing he was out of the race.

When he became aware of that he halted, and dropping on one knee, leveled his gun at the running Tappan. The distance was scarcely sixty yards. His first shot did not allow for Tappan's speed. His second kicked up the gravel in Tappan's face. Then followed three more shots in rapid succession. The man divined that Tappan had a rifle in camp. Then he steadied himself, waiting for the moment when Tappan had to slow down and halt. As Tappan reached his camp and dove for his rifle, the robber took time for his last aim, evidently hoping to get a stationary target. But Tappan did not get up from behind his camp duffel. It had been a habit of his to pile his boxes of supplies and roll of bedding together, and cover them with a canvas. He poked his rifle over the top of this and shot the robber.

Then, leaping up, he ran forward to get sight of the second one. This man began to run along the edge of the gully. Tappan fired rapidly at him. The third shot knocked the fellow down. But he got up, and yelling, as if for succor, he ran off. Tappan got another shot before he disappeared.

"Ahuh!" grunted Tappan, grimly. His keen gaze came back to survey the fallen robber, and then went out over the bench, across the wide mouth of the canyon. Tappan thought he had better utilize time to pack instead of pursuing the fleeing man.

Reloading the rifle, he hurried out to find Jenet. She was coming in to camp.

"Shore you're a treasure, old girl!" ejaculated Tappan.

Never in his life had he packed Jenet, or any other burro, so quickly. His last act was

16

to drink all he could hold, fill his two canteens, and make Jenet drink. Then, rifle in hand, he drove the burro out of camp, round the corner of the red wall, to the wide gateway that opened down into Death Valley.

Tappan looked back more than he looked ahead. And he had traveled down a mile or more before he began to breathe more easily. He had escaped the claim jumpers. Even if they did show up in pursuit now, they could never catch him. Tappan believed he could travel faster and farther than any men of that ilk. But they did not appear. Perhaps the crippled one had not been able to reach his comrades in time. More likely, however, the gang had no taste for a chase in that torrid heat.

Tappan slowed his stride. He was almost as wet with sweat as if he had fallen into the spring. The great beads rolled down his face. And there seemed to be little streams of fire trickling down his breast. But despite this, and his labored panting for breath, not until he halted in the shade of a rocky wall did he realize the heat.

It was terrific. Instantly then he knew he was safe from pursuit. But he knew also that he faced a greater peril than that of robbers. He could fight evil men, but he could not fight this heat.

So he rested there, regaining his breath. Already thirst was acute. Jenet stood near by, watching him. Tappan, with his habit of humanizing the burro, imagined that Jenet looked serious. A moment's thought was enough for Tappan to appreciate the gravity of his situation. He was about to go down into the upper end of Death Valley—a part of that country unfamiliar to him. He must cross it, and also the Funeral Mountains, at a season when a prospector who knew the trails and water holes would have to be forced to undertake it. Tappan had no choice.

His rifle was too hot to hold, so he stuck it in Jenet's pack; and, burdened only by a canteen of water, he set out, driving the burro ahead. Once he looked back up the wide-mouthed canyon. It appeared to smoke with red heat veils. The silence was oppressive.

Presently he turned the last corner that obstructed sight of Death Valley. Tappan had never been appalled by any aspect of the desert, but it was certain that here he halted. Back in his mountain-walled camp the sun had passed behind the high domes, but here it still held most of the valley in its blazing grip. Death Valley looked a ghastly, glaring level of white, over which a strange dull leaden haze drooped like a blanket. Ghosts of mountain peaks appeared to show dim and vague. There was no movement of anything. No wind! The valley was dead. Desolation reigned supreme. Tappan could not see far toward either end of the valley. A few miles of white glare merged at last into a leaden pall. A strong odor, not unlike sulphur, seemed to add weight to the air.

Tappan strode on, mindful that Jenet had decided opinions of her own. She did not want to go straight ahead or to right or left, but back. That was the one direction impossible for Tappan. And he had to resort to a rare measure—that of beating her. But at last Jenet accepted the inevitable and headed down into the stark and naked plain. Soon Tappan reached the margin of the zone of shade cast by the mountain and was now exposed to the sun. The difference seemed tremendous. He had been hot, oppressed, weighted. It was now as if he was burned through his clothes, and walked on red-hot sands.

When Tappan ceased to sweat and his skin became dry, he drank half a canteen of water, and slowed his stride. Inured to desert hardship as he was, he could not long stand this. Jenet did not exhibit any lessening of vigor. In truth what she showed now was an increasing nervousness. It was almost as if she scented an enemy. Tappan never before had such faith in her. Jenet was equal to this task.

With that blazing sun on his back, Tappan felt he was being pursued by a furnace. He was compelled to drink the remaining half of his first canteen of water. Sunset would save him. Two more hours of such insupportable heat would lay him prostrate.

The ghastly glare of the valley took on a reddish tinge. The heat was blinding Tappan. The time came when he walked beside Jenet with a hand on her pack, for his eyes could no longer endure the furnace glare. Even with them closed he knew when the sun sank behind the Panamints. That fire no longer followed him. And the red left his eyelids.

With the sinking of the sun the world of Death Valley changed. It smoked with heat veils. But the intolerable constant burn was gone. The change was so immense that it seemed to have brought coolness.

In the twilight—strange, ghostly, somber, silent as death—Tappan followed Jenet off the sand, down upon the silt and borax level, to the crusty salt. Before dark Jenet halted at a sluggish belt of fluid—acid, it appeared to Tappan. It was not deep. And the bottom felt stable. But Jenet refused to cross. Tappan trusted her judgment more than his own. Jenet headed to the left and followed the course of the strange stream.

Night intervened. A night without stars or sky or sound, hot, breathless, charged with some intangible current! Tappan dreaded the midnight furnace winds of Death Valley. He had never encountered them. He had heard prospectors say that any man caught in Death Valley when these gales blew would never get out to tell the tale. And Jenet seemed to have something on her mind. She was no longer a leisurely, complacent burro.

Tappan imagined Jenet seemed stern. Most assuredly she knew now which way she wanted to travel. It was not easy for Tappan to keep up with her, and ten paces beyond him she was out of sight.

At last Jenet headed the acid wash, and turned across the valley into a field of broken salt crust, like the roughened ice of a river that had broken and jammed, then frozen again. Impossible was it to make even a reasonable headway. It was a zone, however, that eventually gave way to Jenet's instinct for direction. Tappan had long ceased to try to keep his bearings. North, south, east, and west were all the same to him. The night was a blank—the darkness a wall—the silence a terrible menace flung at any living creature. Death Valley had endured them millions of years before living creatures had existed. It was no place for a man.

Tappan was now three hundred and more feet below sea level, in the aftermath of a day that had registered one hundred and forty-five degrees of heat. He knew, when he began to lose thought and balance—when only the primitive instincts directed his bodily machine. And he struggled with all his will power to keep hold of his sense of sight and feeling. He hoped to cross the lower level before the midnight gales began to blow.

Tappan's hope was vain. According to record, once in a long season of intense heat, there came a night when the furnace winds broke their schedule, and began early. The misfortune of Tappan was that he had struck this night.

Suddenly it seemed that the air, sodden with heat, began to move. It had weight. It moved soundlessly and ponderously. But it gathered momentum. Tappen realized what was happening. The blanket of heat generated by the day was yielding to outside pressure. Something had created a movement of the hotter air that must find its way upward, to give place for the cooler air that must find its way down.

Tappan heard the first, low, distant moan of wind and it struck terror to his heart. It did not have an earthly sound. Was that a knell for him? Nothing was surer than the fact that the desert must sooner or later claim him as a victim. Grim and strong, he rebelled against the conviction.

That moan was a forerunner of others, growing louder and longer until the weird sound became continuous. Then the movement of wind was accelerated and began to carry a fine dust. Dark as the night was, it did not hide the pale sheets of dust that moved along the level plain. Tappan's feet felt the slow rise in the floor of the valley. His nose recognized the zone of borax and alkali and niter and sulphur. He had reached the pit of the valley at the time of the furnace winds.

The moan augmented to a roar, coming

like a mighty storm through a forest. It was hellish—like the woeful tide of Acheron. It enveloped Tappan. And the gale bore down in tremendous volume, like a furnace blast. Tappan seemed to feel his body penetrated by a million needles of fire. He seemed to dry up. The blackness of night had a spectral, whitish cast; the gloom was a whirling medium; the valley floor was lost in a sheeted, fiercely seeping stream of silt. Deadly fumes swept by, not lingering long enough to suffocate Tappan. He would gasp and choke— then the poison gas was gone on the gale. But hardest to endure was the heavy body of moving heat. Tappan grew blind, so that he had to hold to Jenet, and stumble along. Every gasping breath was a tortured effort. He could not bear a scarf over his face. His lungs heaved like great leather bellows. His heart pumped like an engine short of fuel. This was the supreme test for his never proven endurance. And he was all but vanquished.

Tappan's sense of sight and smell and hearing failed him. There was left only the sense of touch—a feeling of rope and burro and ground—and an awful insulating pressure upon all his body. His feet marked a change from salty plain to sandy ascent and then to rocky slope. The pressure of wind gradually lessened: the difference in air made life possible; the feeling of being dragged endlessly by Jenet had ceased. Tappan went his limit and fell into oblivion.

When he came to, he was suffering bodily tortures. Sight was dim. But he saw walls of rocks, green growths of mesquite, tamarack, and grass. Jenet was lying down, with her pack flopped to one side. Tappan's dead ears recovered to a strange murmuring, babbling sound. Then he realized his deliverance. Jenet had led him across Death Valley, up into the mountain range, straight to a spring of running water.

Tappan crawled to the edge of the water and drank guardedly, a little at a time. He had to quell terrific craving to drink his fill. Then he crawled to Jenet, and loosening the ropes of her pack, freed her from its burden. Jenet got up, apparently none the worse for her ordeal. She gazed mildly at Tappan, as if to say: "Well, I got you out of that hole."

Tappan returned her gaze. Were they only man and beast, alone in the desert? She seemed magnified to Tappan, no longer a plodding, stupid burro.

"Jenet, you—saved—my life," Tappan tried to enunciate. "I'll never—forget."

Tappan was struck then to a realization of Jenet's service. He was unutterably grateful. Yet the time came when he did forget.

2

Tappan had a weakness common to all prospectors: Any tale of a lost gold mine would excite his interest; and well-known legends of lost mines always obsessed him.

Peg-leg Smith's lost gold mine had lured Tappan to no less than half a dozen trips into the terrible shifting-sand country of southern California. There was no water near the region said to hide this mine of fabulous wealth. Many prospectors had left their bones to bleach white in the sun, finally to be buried by the ever blowing sands. Upon the occasion of Tappan's last escape from this desolate and forbidding desert, he had promised Jenet never to undertake it again. It seemed Tappan promised the faithful burro a good many things. It had been a habit.

When Tappan had a particularly hard experience or perilous adventure, he always took a dislike to the immediate country where it had befallen him. Jenet had dragged him across the Death Valley, through incredible heat and the midnight furnace winds of that strange place; and he had promised her he would never forget how she had saved his life. Nor would he ever go back to Death Valley! He made his way over the Funeral Mountains, worked down through Nevada, and crossed the Rio Colorado above Needles, and entered Arizona. He traveled leisurely, but he kept going, and headed southeast towards Globe. There he cashed one of his six bags of gold, and indulged in the luxury of a complete new outfit. Even Jenet appreciated this fact, for the old outfit would scarcely hold together.

Tappan had the other five bags of gold in his pack; and after hours of hesitation he decided he would not cash them and entrust the money to a bank. He would take care of them. For him the value of this gold amounted to a small fortune. Many plans suggested themselves to Tappan. But in the end he grew weary of them. What did he want with a ranch, or cattle, or an outfitting store, or any of the businesses he now had the means to buy? Towns soon palled on Tappan. People did not long please him. Selfish interest and greed seemed paramount everywhere. Besides, if he acquired a place to take up his time, what would become of Jenet? That question decided him. He packed the burro and once more took to the trails.

A dim, lofty, purple range called alluringly to Tappan. The Superstition Mountains! Somewhere in that purple mass hid the famous treasure called the Lost Dutchman gold mine. Tappan had heard the story often. A Dutch prospector struck gold in the Superstitions. He kept the location secret. When he ran short of money, he would disappear for a few weeks, and then return with bags of gold. Wherever his strike, it assuredly was a rich one. No one ever could trail him or get a word out of him. Time passed. A few years made him old. During this time he conceived a liking for a young man, and eventually confided to him that some day he would tell him the secret of his gold mine. He had drawn a map of the landmarks adjacent to his mine. But he was careful not to put on paper directions how to get there. It chanced that he suddenly fell ill and saw his end was near. Then he summoned the young man who had been so fortunate as to win his regard. Now this individual was a ne'er-do-well, and upon this occasion he was half drunk. The dying Dutchman produced his map, and gave it with verbal directions to the young man. Then he died. When the recipient of this fortune recovered from the effects of liquor, he could not remember all the Dutchman had told him. He tortured himself to remember names and places. But the mine was up in the Superstition Mountains. He never remembered. He never found the lost mine, though he spent his life and died trying. Thus the story passed into the legend of the Lost Dutchman.

Tappan now had his try at finding it. But for him the shifting sands of the southern California desert or even the barren and desolate Death Valley were preferable to this Superstition Range. It was a harder country than the Pinacate of Sonora. Tappan hated cactus, and the Superstitions were full of it. Everywhere stood up the huge *sahuaro*, the giant cacti of the Arizona plateaus, tall like branchless trees, fluted and columnar, beautiful and fascinating to gaze upon, but obnoxious to prospector and burro.

One day from a north slope Tappan saw afar a wonderful country of black timber, above which zigzagged for many miles a yellow, winding rampart of rock. This he took to be the rim of the Mogollon Mesa, one of Arizona's freaks of nature. Something called Tappan. He was forever victim to yearnings for the unattainable. He was tired of heat, glare, dust, bare rock, and thorny cactus. The Lost Dutchman gold mine was a myth. Besides, he did not need any more gold.

Next morning Tappan packed Jenet and worked down off the north slopes of the Superstition Range. That night about sunset he made camp on the bank of a clear brook, with grass and wood in abundance—such a camp site as a prospector dreamed of but seldom found.

Before dark Jenet's long ears told of the advent of strangers. A man and a woman rode down the trail into Tappan's camp. They had poor horses, and led a pack animal that appeared too old and weak to bear up under even the meager pack he carried.

"Howdy," said the man.

Tappan rose from his task to his lofty height and returned the greeting. The man was middle-aged, swarthy, and rugged, a mountaineer, with something about him that Tappan instinctively distrusted. The woman was under thirty, comely in a full-blown way, with rich brown skin and glossy dark hair. She had wide-open black eyes that bent a curious possession-taking gaze upon Tappan.

"Care if we camp with you?" she inquired, and she smiled.

That smile changed Tappan's habit and conviction of a lifetime.

"No indeed. Reckon I'd like a little company," he said.

Very probably Jenet did not understand Tappan's words, but she dropped one ear, and walked out of camp to the green bank.

"Thanks, stranger," replied the woman. "That grub shore smells good." She hesitated a moment, evidently waiting to catch her companion's eye, then she continued. "My name's Madge Beam. He's my brother Jake. . . . Who might you happen to be?"

"I'm Tappan, lone prospector, as you see," replied Tappan.

"Tappan! What's your front handle?" she queried, curiously.

"Fact is, I don't remember," replied Tappan, as he brushed a huge hand through his shaggy hair.

"Ahuh? Any name's good enough."

When she dismounted, Tappan saw that she had a tall, lithe figure, garbed in rider's overalls and boots. She unsaddled her horse with the dexterity of long practice. The saddlebags she carried over to the spot the man Jake had selected to throw the pack.

Tappan heard them talking in low tones. It struck him as strange that he did not have his usual reaction to an invasion of his privacy and solitude. Tappan had thrilled under those black eyes. And now a queer sensation of the unusual rose in him. Bending over his camp-fire tasks he pondered this and that, but mostly the sense of the nearness of a woman. Like most desert men, Tappan knew little of the other sex. A few that he might have been drawn to went out of his wandering life as quickly as they had entered it. This Madge Beam took possession of his thoughts. An evidence of Tappan's preoccupation was the fact that he burned his first batch of biscuits. And Tappan felt proud of his culinary ability. He was on his knees, mixing more flour and water, when the woman spoke from right behind him.

"Tough luck you burned the first pan," she said. "But it's a good turn for your burro. That shore is a burro. Biggest I ever saw."

She picked up the burned biscuits and tossed them over to Jenet. Then she came back to Tappan's side, rather embarrassingly close.

"Tappan, I know how I'll eat, so I ought to ask you to let me help," she said, with a laugh.

"No, I don't need any," replied Tappan. "You sit down on my roll of beddin' there. Must be tired, aren't you?"

"Not so very," she returned. "That is I'm not tired of ridin'." She spoke the second part of this reply in lower tone.

Tappan looked up from his task. The woman had washed her face, brushed her hair, and had put on a skirt—a singularly attractive change. Tappan thought her younger. She was the handsomest woman he had ever seen. The look of her made him clumsy. What eyes she had! They looked through him. Tappan returned to his task, wondering if he was right in his surmise that she wanted to be friendly.

"Jake an' I drove a bunch of cattle to Maricopa," she volunteered. "We sold 'em, an' Jake gambled away most of the money. I couldn't get what I wanted."

"Too bad! So you're ranchers. Once thought I'd like that. Fact is, down there at Globe a few weeks ago I came near buyin' some rancher out an' tryin' the game."

"You did?" Her query had a low, quick eagerness that somehow thrilled Tappan. But he did not look up.

"I'm a wanderer. I'd never do on a ranch."

"But if you had a woman?" Her laugh was subtle and gay.

"A woman! For me? Oh, Lord, no!" ejaculated Tappan, in confusion.

"Why not? Are you a woman hater?"

"I can't say that," replied Tappan, soberly. "It's just—I guess—no woman would have me."

"Faint heart never won fair lady."

Tappan had no reply for that. He surely was making a mess of the second pan of biscuit dough. Manifestly the woman saw this, for with a laugh she plumped down on her knees in front of Tappan, and rolled her sleeves up over shapely brown arms.

"Poor man! Shore you need a woman. Let me show you," she said, and put her hands right down upon Tappan's. The touch gave him a strange thrill. He had to pull his hands away, and as he wiped them with his scarf he looked at her. He seemed compelled to look. She was close to him now, smiling in good nature, a little scornful of man's encroachment upon the house-wifely duties of a woman. A subtle something emanated from her—a more than kindness or gayety. Tappan grasped that it was just the woman of her. And it was going to his head.

"Very well, let's see you show me," he replied, as he rose to his feet.

Just then the brother Jake strolled over, and he had a rather amused and derisive eye for his sister.

"Wal, Tappan, she's not overfond of work, but I reckon she can cook," he said.

Tappan felt greatly relieved at the approach of this brother. And he fell into conversation with him, telling something of his prospecting since leaving Globe, and listening to the man's cattle talk. By and by the woman called, "Come an' get it!" Then they sat down to eat, and, as usual with hungry wayfarers, they did not talk much until appetite was satisfied. Afterward, before the camp fire, they began to talk again, Jake being the most discursive. Tappan conceived the idea that the rancher was rather curious about him, and perhaps wanted to sell his ranch. The woman seemed more thoughtful, with her wide black eyes on the fire.

"Tappan, what way you travelin'?" finally inquired Beam.

"Can't say. I just worked down out of the Superstitions. Haven't any place in mind. Where does this road go?"

"To the Tonto Basin. Ever heard of it?"

"Yes, the name isn't new. What's in this Basin?"

The man grunted. "Tonto once was home for the Apache. It's now got a few sheep an' cattlemen, lots of rustlers. An' say, if you like to hunt bear an' deer, come along with us."

"Thanks. I don't know as I can," returned Tappan, irresolutely. He was not used to such possibilities as this suggested.

Then the woman spoke up. "It's a pretty country. Wild an' different. We live up under the rim rock. There's mineral in the canyons."

Was it that about mineral which decided Tappan or the look in her eyes?

Tappan's world of thought and feeling underwent as great a change as this Tonto Basin differed from the stark desert so long his home. The trail to the log cabin of the Beams climbed many a ridge and slope and foothill, all covered with manzanita, mescal, cedar, and juniper, at last to reach the canyons of the Rim, where lofty pines and spruces lorded it over the under forest of maples and oaks. Though the yellow Rim towered high over the site of the cabin, the altitude was still great, close to seven thousand feet above sea level.

Tappan had fallen in love with this wild wooded and canyoned country. So had Jenet. It was rather funny the way she hung around Tappan, mornings and evenings. She ate luxuriant grass and oak leaves until her sides bulged.

There did not appear to be any flat places in this landscape. Every bench was either up hill or down hill. The Beams had no garden or farm or ranch that Tappan could discover. They raised a few acres of sorghum and corn. Their log cabin was of the most primitive kind, and outfitted poorly. Madge Beam explained that this cabin was their winter abode, and that upon the Rim they had a good house and ranch. Tappan did not inquire closely into anything. If he had interrogated himself, he would have found out that the reason he did not inquire was because he feared something might remove him from the vicinity of Madge Beam. He had thought it strange the Beams avoided wayfarers they had met on the trail, and had gone round a little hamlet Tappan had espied from a hill. Madge Beam, with woman's intuition, had read his mind, and had said: "Jake doesn't get along so well with some of the villagers. An' I've no hankerin' for gun play." That explanation was sufficient for Tappan. He had lived long enough in his wandering years to appreciate that people could have reasons for being solitary.

This trip up into the Rim Rock country bade fair to become Tappan's one and only adventure of the heart. It was not alone the murmuring, clear brook of cold mountain water that enchanted him, nor the stately pines, nor the beautiful silver spruces, nor the wonder of the deep, yellow-walled canyons, so choked with verdure, and haunted by wild creatures. He dared not face his soul, and ask why this dark-eyed woman sought him more and more. Tappan lived in the moment.

He was aware that the few mountaineer neighbors who rode that way rather avoided contact with him. Tappan was not so dense that he did not perceive that the Beams preferred to keep him from outsiders. This perhaps was owing to their desire to sell Tappan the ranch and cattle. Jake offered to let it go at what he called a low figure. Tappan thought it just as well to go out into the forest and hide his bags of gold. He did not trust Jake Beam, and liked less the looks of the men who visited this wilderness ranch. Madge Beam might be related to a rustler, and the associate of rustlers, but that did not necessarily make her a bad woman. Tappan sensed that her attitude was changing, and she seemed to require his respect. At first, all she wanted was his admiration. Tappan's long unused deference for women returned to him, and when he saw that it was having some strange softening effect upon Madge Beam, he redoubled his attentions. They rode and climbed and hunted together. Tappan had pitched his camp not far from the cabin, on a shaded bank of the singing brook. Madge did not leave him much to himself. She was always coming up to his camp, on one pretext or another. Often she would bring two horses, and make Tappan ride with her. Some of these occasions, Tappan saw, occurred while visitors came to the cabin. In three weeks Madge Beam changed from the bold and careless woman who had ridden down into his camp that sunset, to a serious and appealing woman, growing more careful of her person and adornment, and manifestly bearing a burden on her mind.

October came. In the morning white frost glistened on the split-wood shingles of the cabin. The sun soon melted it, and grew warm. The afternoons were still and smoky, melancholy with the enchantment of Indian summer. Tappan hunted wild turkey and deer with Madge, and revived his boyish love of such pursuits. Madge appeared to be a woman of the woods, and had no mean skill with the rifle.

One day they were high on the Rim, with the great timbered basin at their feet. They had come up to hunt deer, but got no farther than the wonderful promontory where before they had lingered.

"Somethin' will happen to me to-day," Madge Beam said, enigmatically.

Tappan never had been much of a talker. But he could listen. The woman unburdened herself this day. She wanted freedom, happiness, a home away from this lonely country, and all the heritage of woman. She confessed it broodingly, passionately. And Tappan recognized truth when he heard it.

He was ready to do all in his power for this woman and believed she knew it. But words and acts of sentiment came hard to him.

"Are you goin' to buy Jake's ranch?" she asked.

"I don't know. Is there any hurry?" returned Tappan.

"I reckon not. But I think I'll settle that," she said, decisively.

"How so?"

"Well, Jake hasn't got any ranch," she answered. And added hastily, "No clear title, I mean. He's only homesteaded one hundred an' sixty acres, an' hasn't proved up on it yet. But don't you say I told you."

"Was Jake aimin' to be crooked?"

"I reckon. . . . An' I was willin' at first. But not now."

Tappan did not speak at once. He saw the woman was in one of her brooding moods. Besides, he wanted to weigh her words. How significant they were! To-day more than ever she had let down. Humility and simplicity seemed to abide with her. And her brooding boded a storm. Tappan's heart swelled in his broad breast. Was life going to dawn rosy and bright for the lonely prospector? He had money to make a home for this woman. What lay in the balance of the hour? Tappan waited, slowly realizing the charged atmosphere.

Madge's somber eyes gazed out over the great void. But, full of thought and passion as they were, they did not see the beauty of that scene. But Tappan saw it. And in some strange sense the color and wildness and sublimity seemed the expression of a new state of his heart. Under him sheered down the ragged and cracked cliffs of the Rim, yellow and gold and gray, full of caves and crevices, ledges for eagles and niches for lions, a thousand feet down to the upward edge of the long green slopes and canyons, and so on down and down into the abyss of forested ravine and ridge, rolling league on league away to the encompassing barrier of purple mountain ranges.

The thickets in the canyons called Tappan's eye back to linger there. How different from the scenes that used to be perpetually in his sight! What riot of color! The tips of the green pines, the crests of the silver spruces, waved about masses of vivid gold of aspen trees, and wonderful cerise and flaming red of maples, and crags of yellow rock, covered with the bronze of frostbitten sumach. Here was autumn and with it the colors of Tappan's favorite season. From below breathed up the low roar of plunging brook; an eagle screeched his wild call; an elk bugled his piercing blast. From the Rim wisps of pine needles blew away on the breeze and fell into the void. A wild country, colorful, beautiful, bountiful. Tappan imagined he could quell his wandering spirit here, with this dark-eyed woman by his side. Never before had Nature so called him. Here was not the cruelty of flinty hardness of the desert. The air was keen and sweet, cold in the shade, warm in the sun. A fragrance of balsam and spruce, spiced with pine, made his breathing a thing of difficulty and delight. How for so many years had he endured vast open spaces without such eye-soothing trees as these? Tappan's back rested against a huge pine that tipped the Rim, and had stood there, stronger than the storms, for many a hundred years. The rock of the promontory was covered with soft brown mats of pine needles. A juniper tree, with its bright green foliage and lilac-colored berries, grew near the pine, and helped to form a secluded little nook, fragrant and somehow haunting. The woman's dark head was close to Tappan, as she sat with her elbows on her knees, gazing down into the basin. Tappan saw the strained tensity of her posture, the heaving of her full bosom. He wondered, while his own emotions, so long darkened, roused to the suspense of that hour.

Suddenly she flung herself into Tappan's arms. The act amazed him. It seemed to have both the passion of a woman and the shame of a girl. Before she hid her face on Tappan's breast he saw how the rich brown had paled, and then flamed.

"Tappan! . . . Take me away. . . . Take me away from here—from that life down there," she cried, in smothered voice.

"Madge, you mean take you away—and marry you?" he replied.

"Oh, yes—yes—marry me, if you love me. . . . I don't see how you can—but you do, don't you?—Say you do."

"I reckon that's what ails me, Madge," he replied, simply.

"*Say* so, then," she burst out.

"All right, I do," said Tappan, with heavy breath. "Madge, words don't come easy for me. . . . But I think you're wonderful, an' I want you. I haven't dared hope for that, till now. I'm only a wanderer. But it'd be heaven to have you—my wife—an' make a home for you."

"Oh—Oh!" she returned, wildly, and lifted herself to cling round his neck, and to kiss him. "You give me joy. . . . Oh, Tappan, I love you. I never loved any man before. I know now. . . . An' I'm not wonderful—or good. But I love you."

The fire of her lips and the clasp of her arms worked havoc in Tappan. No woman had ever loved him, let alone embraced him. To awake suddenly to such rapture as this made him strong and rough in his response. Then all at once she seemed to collapse in his arms and to begin to weep. He feared he had offended or hurt her, and was clumsy in his contrition. Presently she replied:

"Pretty soon—I'll make you—beat me. It's your love—your honesty—that's shamed me. . . . Tappan, I was party to a trick to—

sell you a worthless ranch. . . . I agreed to—
try to make you love me—to fool you—cheat
you. . . . But I've fallen in love with you.—An'
my God, I care more for your love—your respect—than for my life. I can't go on with it.
I've double-crossed Jake, an' all of them. . . .
Now, am I worth lovin'? Am I worth havin'?"

"More than ever, dear," he said.

"You will take me away?"

"Anywhere—any time, the sooner the better."

She kissed him passionately, and then, dis-
engaging herself from his arms, she knelt
and gazed earnestly at him. "I've not told all.
I will some day. But I swear now on my
soul—I'll be what you think me."

"Madge, you needn't say all that. If you
love me—it's enough. More than I ever
dreamed of."

"You're a man. Oh, why didn't I meet you
when I was eighteen instead of now—twenty-
eight, an' all that between. . . . But enough. A
new life begins here for me. We must plan."

"You make the plans an' I'll act on them."

For a moment she was tense and silent,
head bowed, hands shut tight. Then she
spoke:

"To-night we'll slip away. You make a light
pack, that'll go on your saddle. I'll do the
same. We'll hide the horses out near where
the trail crosses the brook. An' we'll run off—
ride out of the country."

Tappan in turn tried to think, but the whirl

of his mind made any reason difficult. This dark-eyed, full-bosomed woman loved him, had surrendered herself, asked only his protection. The thing seemed marvelous. Yet she knelt there, those dark eyes on him, infinitely more appealing than ever, haunting with some mystery of sadness and fear he could not divine.

Suddenly Tappan remembered Jenet.

"I must take Jenet," he said.

That startled her. "Jenet—Who's she?"

"My burro."

"Your burro. You can't travel fast with that pack beast. We'll be trailed, an' we'll have to go fast. . . . You can't take the burro."

Then Tappan was startled. "What! Can't take Jenet?—Why, I—I couldn't get along without her."

"Nonsense. What's a burro? We must ride fast—do you hear?"

"Madge, I'm afraid I—I must take Jenet with me," he said, soberly.

"It's impossible. I can't go if you take her. I tell you I've got to get away. If you want *me* you'll have to leave your precious Jenet behind."

Tappan bowed his head to the inevitable. After all, Jenet was only a beast of burden. She would run wild on the ridges and soon forget him and have no need of him. Something strained in Tappan's breast. He did not see clearly here. This woman was worth more than all else to him.

"I'm stupid, dear," he said. "You see I never before ran off with a beautiful woman. . . . Of course my burro must be left behind."

Elopement, if such it could be called, was easy for them. Tappan did not understand why Madge wanted to be so secret about it. Was she not free? But then, he reflected, he did not know the circumstances she feared. Besides, he did not care. Possession of the woman was enough.

Tappan made his small pack, the weight of which was considerable owing to his bags of gold. This he tied on his saddle. It bothered him to leave most of his new outfit scattered around his camp. What would Jenet think of that? He looked for her, but for once she did not come in at meal time. Tappan thought this was singular. He could not remember when Jenet had been far from his camp at sunset. Somehow Tappan was glad.

After he had his supper, he left his utensils and supplies as they happened to be, and strode away under the trees to the trysting-place where he was to meet Madge. To his surprise she came before dark, and, unused as he was to the complexity and emotional nature of a woman, he saw that she was strangely agitated. Her face was pale. Almost a fury burned in her black eyes. When she came up to Tappan, and embraced him, almost fiercely, he felt that he was about to learn more of the nature of womankind. She thrilled him to his depths.

"Lead out the horses an' don't make any noise," she whispered.

Tappan complied, and soon he was mounted, riding behind her on the trail. It surprised him that she headed down country, and traveled fast. Moreover, she kept to a trail that continually grew rougher. They came to a road, which she crossed, and kept on through darkness and brush so thick that Tappan could not see the least sign of a trail. And at length anyone could have seen that Madge had lost her bearings. She appeared to know the direction she wanted, but traveling upon it was impossible, owing to the increasingly cut-up and brushy ground. They had to turn back, and seemed to be hours finding the road. Once Tappan fancied he heard the thud of hoofs other than those made by their own horses. Here Madge acted strangely, and where she had been obsessed by desire to hurry she now seemed to have grown weary. She turned her horse south on the road. Tappan was thus enabled to ride beside her. But they talked very little. He was satisfied with the fact of being with her on the way out of the country. Some time in the night they reached an old log shack by the roadside. Here Tappan suggested they halt, and get some sleep before dawn. The morrow would mean a long hard day.

"Yes, to-morrow will be hard," replied

Madge, as she faced Tappan in the gloom. He could see her big dark eyes on him. Her tone was not one of a hopeful woman. Tappan pondered over this. But he could not understand, because he had no idea how a woman ought to act under such circumstances. Madge Beam was a creature of moods. Only the day before, on the ride down from the Rim, she had told him with a laugh that she was likely to love him madly one moment and scratch his eyes out the next. How could he know what to make of her? Still, an uneasy feeling began to stir in Tappan.

They dismounted, and unsaddled the horses. Tappan took his pack and put it aside. Something frightened the horses. They bolted down the road.

"Head them off," cried the woman, hoarsely.

Even on the instant her voice sounded strained to Tappan, as if she were choked. But, realizing the absolute necessity of catching the horses, he set off down the road on a run. And he soon succeeded in heading off the animal he had ridden. The other one, however, was contrary and cunning. When Tappan would endeavor to get ahead, it would trot briskly on. Yet it did not go so fast but what Tappan felt sure he would soon catch it. Thus walking and running, he put some distance between him and the cabin before he realized that he could not head off the wary beast. Much perturbed in mind, Tappan hurried back.

Upon reaching the cabin Tappan called to Madge. No answer! He could not see her in the gloom nor the horse he had driven back. Only silence brooded there. Tappan called again. Still no answer! Perhaps Madge had succumbed to weariness and was asleep. A search of the cabin and vicinity failed to yield any sign of her. But it disclosed the fact that Tappan's pack was gone.

Suddenly he sat down, quite overcome. He had been duped. What a fierce pang tore his heart! But it was for loss of the woman—not the gold. He was stunned, and then sick with bitter misery. Only then did Tappan realize the meaning of love and what it had done to him. The night wore on, and he sat there in the dark and cold and stillness until the gray dawn told him of the coming of day.

The light showed his saddle where he had left it. Near by lay one of Madge's gloves. Tappan's keen eye sighted a bit of paper sticking out of the glove. He picked it up. It was a leaf out of a little book he had seen her carry, and upon it was written in lead pencil:

"I am Jake's wife, not his sister. I double-crossed him an' ran off with you an' would have gone to hell for you. But Jake an' his gang suspected me. They were close on our trail. I couldn't shake them. So here I chased off the horses an' sent you after them. It was the only way I could save your life."

Tappan tracked the thieves to Globe. There he learned they had gone to Phoenix—three men and one woman. Tappan had money on his person. He bought horse and saddle, and, setting out for Phoenix, he let his passion to kill grow with the miles and hours. At Phoenix he learned Beam had cashed the gold—twelve thousand dollars. So much of a fortune! Tappan's fury grew. The gang separated here. Beam and his wife took stage for Tucson. Tappan had no trouble in trailing their movements.

Gambling dives and inns and freighting posts and stage drivers told the story of the Beams and their ill-gotten gold. They went on to California, down into Tappan's country, to Yuma, and El Cajon, and San Diego. Here Tappan lost track of the woman. He could not find that she had left San Diego, nor any trace of her there. But Jake Beam had killed a Mexican in a brawl and had fled across the line.

Tappan gave up for the time being the chase of Beam, and bent his efforts to find the woman. He had no resentment toward Madge. He only loved her. All that winter he searched San Diego. He made of himself a peddler as a ruse to visit houses. But he never found a trace of her. In the spring he wandered back to Yuma, raking over the old clues, and so on back to Tucson and Phoenix.

This year of dream and love and passion and despair and hate made Tappan old. His great strength and endurance were not yet impaired, but something of his spirit had died out of him.

One day he remembered Jenet. "My burro!" he soliloquized. "I had forgotten her. . . . Jenet!"

Then it seemed a thousand impulses merged in one drove him to face the long road toward the Rim Rock country. To remember Jenet was to grow doubtful. Of course she would be gone. Stolen or dead or wandered off! But then who could tell what Jenet might do? Tappan was both called and driven. He was a poor wanderer again. His outfit was a pack he carried on his shoulder. But while he could walk he would keep on until he found that last camp where he had deserted Jenet.

October was coloring the canyon slopes when he reached the shadow of the great wall of yellow rock. The cabin where the Beams had lived—or had claimed they lived—was a fallen ruin, crushed by snow. Tappan saw other signs of a severe winter and heavy snowfall. No horse or cattle tracks showed in the trails.

To his amaze his camp was much as he had left it. The stone fireplace, the iron pots, appeared to be in the same places. The boxes that had held his supplies were lying here and there. And his canvas tarpaulin, little the worse for wear of the elements, lay on the ground under the pine where he had slept. If any man had visited this camp in a year he had left no sign of it.

Suddenly Tappan espied a hoof track in the dust. A small track—almost oval in shape—fresh! Tappan thrilled through all his being.

"Jenet's track, so help me God!" he murmured.

He found more of them, made that morning. And, keen now as never before on her trail, he set out to find her. The tracks led up the canyon. Tappan came out into a little grassy clearing, and there stood Jenet, as he had seen her thousands of times. She had both long ears up high. She seemed to stare out of that meek, gray face. And then one of the long ears flopped over and drooped. Such perhaps was the expression of her recognition.

Tappan strode up to her.

"Jenet—old girl—you hung round camp—waitin' for me, didn't you?" he said, huskily, and his big hands fondled her long ears.

Yes, she had waited. She, too, had grown old. She was gray. The winter of that year had been hard. What had she lived on when the snow lay so deep? There were lion scratches on her back, and scars on her legs. She had fought for her life.

"Jenet, a man can never always tell about a burro," said Tappan. "I trained you to hang round camp an' wait till I came back. . . . 'Tappan's burro,' the desert rats used to say! An' they'd laugh when I bragged how you'd stick to me where most men would quit. But brag as I did, I never knew you, Jenet. An' I left you—an' forgot. Jenet, it takes a human bein'—a man—a woman—to be faithless. An' it takes a dog or a horse or a burro to be great. . . . Beasts? I wonder now. . . . Well, old pard, we're goin' down the trail together, an' from this day on Tappan begins to pay his debt."

3

TAPPAN NEVER AGAIN HAD THE OLD *WANDERLUST* for the stark and naked desert. Something had transformed him. The green and fragrant forests, the brown-aisled, pine-matted woodlands, the craggy promontories and the great colored canyons, the cold granite water springs of the Tonto seemed vastly preferable to the heat and dust and glare and the emptiness of the waste lands. But there was more. The ghost of his strange and only love kept pace with his wandering steps, a spirit that hovered with him as his shadow. Madge Beam, whatever she had been, had showed to him the power of love to refine and ennoble. Somehow he felt closer to her here in the cliff country where his passion had been born. Somehow she seemed nearer to him here than in all those places he had tracked her.

So from a prospector searching for gold Tappan became a hunter, seeking only the means to keep soul and body together. And all he cared for was his faithful burro Jenet, and the loneliness and silence of the forest land.

He was to learn that the Tonto was a hard country in many ways, and bitterly so in winter. Down in the brakes of the basin it was mild in winter, the snow did not lie long, and ice seldom formed. But up on the Rim, where Tappan always lingered as long as possible, the storm king of the north held full sway. Fifteen feet of snow and zero weather were the rule in dead of winter.

An old native once warned Tappan: "See hyar, friend, I reckon you'd better not get caught up in the Rim Rock country in one of our big storms. Fer if you do you'll never get out."

It was a way of Tappan's to follow his inclinations, regardless of advice. He had weathered the terrible midnight storm of hot wind in Death Valley. What were snow and cold to him? Late autumn on the Rim was the most perfect and beautiful of seasons. He had seen the forest land brown and darkly green one day, and the next burdened with white snow. What a transfiguration! Then when the sun loosened the white mantling on the pines, and they had shed their burdens in drifting dust of white, and rainbowed mists of melting snow, and avalanches sliding off the branches, there would be left only the wonderful white floor of the woodland. The great rugged brown tree trunks appeared mightier and statelier in the contrast; and the green of foliage, the russet of oak leaves, the gold of the aspens, turned the forest into a world enchanting to the desert-seared eyes of this wanderer.

With Tappan the years sped by. His mind grew old faster than his body. Every season saw him lonelier. He had a feeling, a vague illusive foreshadowing that his bones, instead of bleaching on the desert sands, would mingle with the pine mats and the soft fragrant moss of the forest. The idea was pleasant to Tappan.

One afternoon he was camped in Pine Canyon, a timber-sloped gorge far back from the Rim. November was well on. The fall had been singularly open and fair, with not a single storm. A few natives happening across Tappan had remarked casually that such autumns sometimes were not to be trusted.

This late afternoon was one of Indian summer beauty and warmth. The blue haze in the canyon was not all the blue smoke from Tappan's camp fire. In a narrow park of grass not far from camp Jenet grazed peacefully with elk and deer. Wild turkeys lingered there, loth to seek their winter quarters down in the basin. Gray squirrels and red squirrels barked and frisked, and dropped the pine and spruce cones, with thud and thump, on all the slopes.

Before dark a stranger rode into Tappan's camp, a big man of middle age, whose magnificent physique impressed even Tappan. He was a rugged, bearded giant, wide-eyed and of pleasant face. He had no outfit, no horse, not even a gun.

"Lucky for me I smelled your smoke," he said. "Two days for me without grub."

"Howdy, stranger," was Tappan's greeting. "Are you lost?"

"Yes an' no. I could find my way out down over the Rim, but it's not healthy down there for me. So I'm hittin' north."

"Where's your horse an' pack?"

"I reckon they're with the gang thet took more of a fancy to them than me."

"Ahuh! You're welcome here, stranger," replied Tappan. "I'm Tappan."

"Ha! Heard of you. I'm Jess Blade, of anywhere. An' I'll say, Tappan, I was an honest man till I hit the Tonto."

His laugh was frank, for all its note of grimness. Tappan liked the man, and sensed one who would be a good friend and bad foe.

"Come an' eat. My supplies are peterin' out, but there's plenty of meat."

Blade ate, indeed, as a man starved, and did not seem to care if Tappan's supplies were low. He did not talk. After the meal he craved a pipe and tobacco. Then he smoked in silence, in a slow realizing content. The morrow had no fears for him. The flickering ruddy light from the camp fire shone on his strong face. Tappan saw in him the drifter, the drinker, the brawler, a man with good in him, but over whom evil passion or temper dominated. Presently he smoked the pipe out, and with reluctant hand knocked out the ashes and returned it to Tappan.

"I reckon I've some news thet'd interest you," he said.

"You have?" queried Tappan.

"Yes, if you're the Tappan who tried to run off with Jake Beam's wife."

"Well, I'm that Tappan. But I'd like to say I didn't know she was married."

"Shore, I know thet. So does everybody in the Tonto. You were just meat for thet Beam gang. They had played the trick before. But accordin' to what I hear thet trick was the last fer Madge Beam. She never came back to this country. An' Jake Beam, when he was drunk, owned up thet she'd left him in California. Some hint at worse. Fer Jake Beam came back a harder man. Even his gang said thet."

"Is he in the Tonto now?" queried Tappan, with a thrill of fire along his veins.

"Yep, thar fer keeps," replied Blade, grimly. "Somebody shot him."

"Ahuh!" exclaimed Tappan with a deep

breath of relief. There came a sudden cooling of the heat of his blood.

After that there was a long silence. Tappan dreamed of the woman who had loved him. Blade brooded over the camp fire. The wind moaned fitfully in the lofty pines on the slope. A wolf mourned as if in hunger. The stars appeared to obscure their radiance in haze.

"Reckon thet wind sounds like storm," observed Blade, presently.

"I've heard it for weeks now," replied Tappan.

"Are you a woodsman?"

"No, I'm a desert man."

"Wal, you take my hunch an' hit the trail fer low country."

This was well meant, and probably sound advice, but it alienated Tappan. He had really liked this hearty-voiced stranger. Tappan thought moodily of his slowly ingrowing mind, of the narrowness of his soul. He was past interest in his fellow men. He lived with a dream. The only living creature he loved was a lop-eared, lazy burro, growing old in contentment. Nevertheless that night Tappan shared one of his two blankets.

In the morning the gray dawn broke, and the sun rose without its brightness of gold. There was a haze over the blue sky. Thin, swift-moving clouds scudded up out of the southwest. The wind was chill, the forest shaggy and dark, the birds and squirrels were silent.

"Wal, you'll break camp to-day," asserted Blade.

"Nope. I'll stick it out yet a while," returned Tappan.

"But, man, you might get snowed in, an' up hyar thet's serious."

"Ahuh! Well, it won't bother me. An' there's nothin' holdin' you."

"Tappan, it's four days' walk down out of this woods. If a big snow set in, how'd I make it?"

"Then you'd better go out over the Rim," suggested Tappan.

"No. I'll take my chance the other way. But are you meanin' you'd rather not have me with you? Fer you can't stay hyar."

Tappan was in a quandary.

Some instinct bade him tell the man to go. Not empty-handed, but to go. But this was selfish, and entirely unlike Tappan as he remembered himself of old. Finally he spoke:

"You're welcome to half my outfit—go or stay."

"Thet's mighty square of you, Tappan," responded the other, feelingly. "Have you a burro you'll give me?"

"No, I've only one."

"Ha! Then I'll have to stick with you till you leave."

No more was said. They had breakfast in a strange silence. The wind brooded its secret in the tree tops. Tappan's burro strolled into camp, and caught the stranger's eye.

"Wal, thet's shore a fine burro," he observed. "Never saw the like."

Tappan performed his camp tasks. And then there was nothing to do but sit around the fire. Blade evidently waited for the increasing menace of storm to rouse Tappan to decision. But the graying over of sky and the increase of wind did not affect Tappan. What did he wait for? The truth of his thoughts was that he did not like the way Jenet remained in camp. She was waiting to be packed. She knew they ought to go. Tappan yielded to a perverse devil of stubbornness. The wind brought a cold mist, then a flurry of wet snow. Tappan gathered firewood, a large quantity. Blade saw this and gave voice to earnest fears. But Tappan paid no heed. By nightfall sleet and snow began to fall steadily. The men fashioned a rude shack of spruce boughs, ate their supper, and went to bed early.

It worried Tappan that Jenet stayed right in camp. He lay awake a long time. The wind rose, and moaned through the forest. The sleet failed, and a soft, steady downfall of snow gradually set in. Tappan fell asleep. When he awoke it was to see a forest of white. The trees were mantled with blankets of wet snow, the ground covered two feet on a level. But the clouds appeared to be gone, the sky was blue, the storm over. The sun came up warm and bright.

"It'll all go in a day," said Tappan.

"If this was early October I'd agree with you," replied Blade. "But it's only makin' fer another storm. Can't you hear thet wind?"

Tappan only heard the whispers of his dreams. By now the snow was melting off the pines, and rainbows shone everywhere. Little patches of snow began to drop off the south branches of the pines and spruces, and then larger patches, until by mid-afternoon white streams and avalanches were falling everywhere. All of the snow, except in shaded places on the north sides of trees, went that day, and half of that on the ground. Next day it thinned out more, until Jenet was finding the grass and moss again. That afternoon the tell-tale thin clouds raced up out of the southwest and the wind moaned its menace.

"Tappan, let's pack an' hit it out of hyar," appealed Blade, anxiously. "I know this county. Mebbe I'm wrong, of course, but it feels like storm. Winter's comin' shore."

"Let her come," replied Tappan, imperturbably.

"Say, do you want to get snowed in?" demanded Blade, out of patience.

"I might like a little spell of it, seein' it'd be new to me," replied Tappan.

"But man, if you ever get snowed in hyar you can't get out."

"That burro of mine could get me out."

"You're crazy. Thet burro couldn't go a hundred feet. What's more, you'd have to kill her an' eat her."

Tappan bent a strange gaze upon his companion, but made no reply. Blade began to pace up and down the small bare patch of ground before the camp fire. Manifestly, he was in a serious predicament. That day he seemed subtly to change, as did Tappan. Both answered to their peculiar instincts, Blade to that of self-preservation, and Tappan, to something like indifference. Tappan held fate in defiance. What more could happen to him?

Blade broke out again, in eloquent persuasion, giving proof of their peril, and from that he passed to amaze and then to strident anger. He cursed Tappan for a nature-loving idiot.

"An' I'll tell you what," he ended. "When mornin' comes I'll take some of your grub an' hit it out of hyar, storm or no storm."

But long before dawn broke that resolution of Blade's had become impracticable. Both men were awakened by a roar of storm through the forest, no longer a moan, but a marching roar, with now a crash and then a shriek of gale! By the light of the smouldering camp fire Tappan saw a whirling pall of snow, great flakes as large as feathers. Morning disclosed the setting in of a fierce mountain storm, with two feet of snow already on the ground, and the forest lost in a blur of white.

"I was wrong," called Tappan to his companion. "What's best to do now?"

"You damned fool!" yelled Blade. "We've got to keep from freezin' an' starvin' till the storm ends an' a crust comes on the snow."

For three days and three nights the blizzard continued, unabated in its fury. It took the men hours to keep a space cleared for their camp site, which Jenet shared with them. On the fourth day the storm ceased, the clouds broke away, the sun came out. And the temperature dropped to zero. Snow on the level just topped Tappan's lofty stature, and in drifts it was ten and fifteen feet deep. Winter had set in without compromise. The forest became a solemn, still, white world. But now Tappan had no time to dream. Dry firewood was hard to find under the snow. It was possible to cut down one of the dead trees on the slope, but impossible to pack sufficient wood to the camp. They had to burn green wood. Then the fashioning of snowshoes took much time. Tappan had no knowledge of such footgear. He could only help Blade. The men were encouraged by the piercing cold forming a crust on the snow. But just as they were about to pack and venture forth, the weather moderated, the crust refused to hold their weight, and another foot of snow fell.

"Why in hell didn't you kill an elk?" demanded Blade, sullenly. He had become darkly sinister. He knew the peril and he loved life. "Now we'll have to kill an' eat your precious Jenet. An' mebbe she won't furnish meat enough to last till this snow weather stops an' a good freeze'll make travelin' possible."

"Blade, you shut up about killin' an' eatin' my burro Jenet," returned Tappan, in a voice that silenced the other.

Thus instinctively these men became enemies. Blade thought only of himself. Tappan had forced upon him a menace to the life of his burro. For himself Tappan had not one thought.

Tappan's supplies ran low. All the bacon and coffee were gone. There was only a small haunch of venison, a bag of beans, a sack of flour, and a small quantity of salt left.

"If a crust freezes on the snow an' we can pack that flour, we'll get out alive," said Blade. "But we can't take the burro."

Another day of bright sunshine softened the snow on the southern exposures, and a night of piercing cold froze a crust that would bear a quick step of man.

"It's our only chance—an' damn slim at thet," declared Blade.

Tappan allowed Blade to choose the time and method, and supplies for the start to get out of the forest. They cooked all the beans and divided them in two sacks. Then they baked about five pounds of biscuits for each of them. Blade showed his cunning when he chose the small bag of salt for himself and let Tappan take the tobacco. This quantity of food and a blanket for each Blade declared to be all they could pack. They argued over the guns, and in the end Blade compromised on the rifle, agreeing to let Tappan carry that on a possible chance of killing a deer or elk. When this matter had been decided, Blade significantly began putting on his rude snowshoes, that had been constructed from pieces of Tappan's boxes and straps and burlap sacks.

"Reckon they won't last long," muttered Blade.

Meanwhile Tappan fed Jenet some biscuits and then began to strap a tarpaulin on her back.

"What you doin'?" queried Blade, suddenly.

"Gettin' Jenet ready," replied Tappan.

"Ready! For what?"

"Why, to go with us."

"Hell!" shouted Blade, and he threw up his hands in helpless rage.

Tappan felt a depth stirred within him. He lost his late taciturnity and silent aloofness fell away from him. Blade seemed on the moment no longer an enemy. He loomed as an aid to the saving of Jenet. Tappan burst into speech.

"I can't go without her. It'd never enter my head. Jenet's mother was a good faithful burro. I saw Jenet born way down there on the Rio Colorado. She wasn't strong. An' I had to wait for her to be able to walk. An' she grew up. Her mother died, an' Jenet an' me packed it alone. She wasn't no ordinary burro. She learned all I taught her. She was different. But I treated her same as any burro. An' she grew with the years. Desert men said there never was such a burro as Jenet. Called her Tappan's burro, an' tried to borrow an' buy an' steal her. . . . How many times in ten years Jenet has done me a good turn I can't remember. But she saved my life. She dragged me out of Death Valley. . . . An' then I forgot my debt. I ran off with a woman an' left Jenet to wait as she had been trained to wait. . . . Well, I got back in time. . . . An' now I'll not leave her. It may be strange to you, Blade, me carin' this way. Jenet's only a burro. But I won't leave her."

"Man, you talk like thet lazy lop-eared burro was a woman," declared Blade, in disgusted astonishment.

"I don't know women, but I reckon Jenet's more faithful than most of them."

"Wal, of all the stark, starin' fools I ever run into you're the worst."

"Fool or not, I know what I'll do," retorted Tappan. The softer mood left him swiftly.

"Haven't you sense enough to see thet we can't travel with your burro?" queried Blade, patiently controlling his temper. "She has little hoofs, sharp as knives. She'll cut through the crust. She'll break through in places. An' we'll have to stop to haul her out—mebbe break through ourselves. Thet would make us longer gettin' out."

"Long or short we'll take her."

Then Blade confronted Tappan as if suddenly unmasking his true meaning. His patient explanation meant nothing. Under no circumstances would he ever have consented to an attempt to take Jenet out of that snowbound wilderness. His eyes gleamed.

"We've a hard pull to get out alive. An' hard-workin' men in winter must have meat to eat."

Tappan slowly straightened up to look at the speaker.

"What do you mean?"

For answer Blade jerked his hand backward and downward, and when it swung into sight it held Tappan's worn and shining rifle. Then Blade, with deliberate force, that showed the nature of the man, worked the lever and threw a shell into the magazine. All the while his eyes were fastened on Tappan. His face seemed that of another man, evil, relentless, inevitable in his spirit to preserve his own life at any cost.

"I mean to kill your burro," he said, in voice that suited his look and manner.

"No!" cried Tappan, shocked into an instant of appeal.

"Yes, I am, an' I'll bet, by God, before we

get out of hyar you'll be glad to eat some of her meat!"

That roused the slow-gathering might of Tappan's wrath.

"I'd starve to death before I'd—I'd kill that burro, let alone eat her."

"Starve an' be damned!" shouted Blade, yielding to rage.

Jenet stood right behind Tappan, in her posture of contented repose, with one long ear hanging down over her gray meek face.

"You'll have to kill me first," answered Tappan, sharply.

"I'm good fer anythin'—if you push me," returned Blade, stridently.

As he stepped aside, evidently so he could have unobstructed aim at Jenet, Tappan leaped forward and knocked up the rifle as it was discharged. The bullet sped harmlessly over Jenet. Tappan heard it thud into a tree. Blade uttered a curse. And as he lowered the rifle in sudden deadly intent, Tappan grasped the barrel with his left hand. Then, clenching his right, he struck Blade a sodden blow in the face. Only Blade's hold on the rifle prevented him from falling. Blood streamed from his nose and mouth. He bellowed in hoarse fury,

"I'll kill you—fer thet!"

Tappan opened his clenched teeth: "No, Blade—you're not man enough."

Then began a terrific struggle for possession of the rifle. Tappan beat at Blade's face with his sledge-hammer fist. But the strength of the other made it imperative that he use both hands to keep his hold on the rifle. Wrestling and pulling and jerking, the men tore round the snowy camp, scattering the camp fire, knocking down the brush shelter. Blade had surrendered to a wild frenzy. He hissed his maledictions. His was the brute lust to kill an enemy that thwarted him. But Tappan was grim and terrible in his restraint. His battle was to save Jenet. Nevertheless, there mounted in him the hot physical sensations of the savage. The contact of flesh, the smell and sight of Blade's blood, the violent action, the beastly mien of his foe, changed the fight to one for its own sake. To conquer this foe, to rend him and beat him and beat him down, blow on blow!

Tappan felt instinctively that he was the stronger. Suddenly he exerted all his muscular force into one tremendous wrench. The rifle broke, leaving the steel barrel in his hands, the wooden stock in Blade's. And it was the quicker-witted Blade who used his weapon first to advantage. One swift blow knocked Tappan down. As he was about to follow it up with another, Tappan kicked his opponent's feet from under him. Blade sprawled in the snow, but was up again as quickly as Tappan. They made at each other, Tappan waiting to strike, and Blade raining blows on Tappan. These were heavy blows aimed at his head, but which he contrived to receive on his arms and the rifle barrel he brandished. For a few moments Tappan stood up under a beating that would have felled a lesser man. His own blood blinded him. Then he swung his heavy weapon. The blow broke Blade's left arm. Like a wild beast, he screamed in pain; and then, without guard, rushed in, too furious for further caution. Tappan met the terrible onslaught as before, and watching his chance, again swung the rifle barrel. This time, so supreme was the force, it battered down Blade's arm and crushed his skull. He died on his feet— ghastly and horrible change!—and swaying backward, he fell into the upbanked wall of snow, and went out of sight, except for his boots, one of which still held the crude snowshoe.

Tappan stared, slowly realizing.

"Ahuh, stranger Blade!" he ejaculated, gazing at the hole in the snow bank where his foe had disappeared. "You were goin' to—kill an' eat—Tappan's burro!"

Then he sighted the bloody rifle barrel, and cast it from him. He became conscious of injuries which needed attention. But he could do little more than wash off the blood and bind up his head. Both arms and hands were badly bruised, and beginning to swell. But fortunately no bones had been broken.

Tappan finished strapping the tarpaulin upon the burro; and, taking up both his and

Blade's supply of food, he called out, "Come on, Jenet."

Which way to go! Indeed, there was no more choice for him than there had been for Blade. Towards the Rim the snowdrift would be deeper and impassable. Tappan realized that the only possible chance for him was down hill. So he led Jenet out of camp without looking back once. What was it that had happened? He did not seem to be the same Tappan that had dreamily tramped into this woodland.

A deep furrow in the snow had been made by the men packing firewood into camp. At the end of this furrow the wall of snow stood higher than Tappan's head. To get out on top without breaking the crust presented a problem. He lifted Jenet up, and was relieved to see that the snow held her. But he found a different task in his own case. Returning to camp, he gathered up several of the long branches of spruce that had been part of the shelter, and carrying them out he laid them against the slant of snow he had to surmount, and by their aid he got on top. The crust held him.

Elated and with revived hope, he took up Jenet's halter and started off. Walking with his rude snowshoes was awkward. He had to go slowly, and slide them along the crust. But he progressed. Jenet's little steps kept her even with him. Now and then one of her sharp hoofs cut through, but not to hinder her particularly. Right at the start Tappan observed a singular something about Jenet. Never until now had she been dependent upon him. She knew it. Her intelligence apparently told her that if she got out of this snow-bound wilderness it would be owing to the strength and reason of her master.

Tappan kept to the north side of the canyon, where the snow crust was strongest. What he must do was to work up to the top of the canyon slope, and then keeping to the ridge travel north along it, and so down out of the forest.

Travel was slow. He soon found he had to pick his way. Jenet appeared to be absolutely unable to sense either danger or safety. Her experience had been of the rock confines and the drifting sands of the desert. She walked where Tappan led her. And it seemed to Tappan that her trust in him, her reliance upon him, were pathetic.

"Well, old girl," said Tappan to her, "it's a horse of another color now—hey?"

At length he came to a wide part of the canyon, where a bench of land led to a long gradual slope, thickly studded with small pines. This appeared to be fortunate, and turned out to be so, for when Jenet broke through the crust Tappan had trees and branches to hold to while he hauled her out. The labor of climbing that slope was such that Tappan began to appreciate Blade's absolute refusal to attempt getting Jenet out.

Dusk was shadowing the white aisles of the forest when Tappen ascended to a level. He had not traveled far from camp, and the fact struck a chill upon his heart.

To go on in the dark was foolhardy. So Tappan selected a thick spruce, under which there was a considerable depression in the snow, and here made preparations to spend the night. Unstrapping the tarpaulin, he spread it on the snow. All the lower branches of this giant of the forest were dead and dry. Tappan broke off many and soon had a fire. Jenet nibbled at the moss on the trunk of the spruce tree. Tappan's meal consisted of beans, biscuits, and a ball of snow, that he held over the fire to soften. He saw to it that Jenet fared as well as he. Night soon fell, strange and weirdly white in the forest, and piercingly cold. Tappan needed the fire. Gradually it melted the snow and made a hole, down to the ground. Tappan rolled up in the tarpaulin and soon fell asleep.

In three days Tappan traveled about fifteen miles, gradually descending, until the snow crust began to fail to hold Jenet. Then whatever had been his difficulties before, they were now magnified a hundredfold. As soon as the sun was up, somewhat softening the snow, Jenet began to break through. And often when Tappan began hauling her out he broke through himself. This exertion was killing even to a man of Tappan's physical prowess. The endurance to resist heat and flying dust and dragging sand seemed another kind from that needed to toil on in this snow. The endless snow-bound forest began to be hideous to Tappan. Cold, lonely, dreary, white, mournful—the kind of ghastly and ghostly winter land that had been the terror of Tappan's boyish dreams! He loved the sun—the open. This forest had deceived him. It was a wall of ice. As he toiled on, the state of his mind gradually and subtly changed in all except the fixed and absolute will to save Jenet. In some places he carried her.

The fourth night found him dangerously near the end of his stock of food. He had been generous with Jenet. But now, considering that he had to do more work than she, he diminished her share. On the fifth day Jenet broke through the snow crust so often that Tappan realized how utterly impossible it was for her to get out of the woods by her own efforts. Therefore Tappan hit upon the plan of making her lie on the tarpaulin, so that he could drag her. The tarpaulin doubled once did not make a bad sled. All the rest of that day Tappan hauled her. And so all the rest of the next day he toiled on, hands behind him, clutching the canvas, head and shoulders bent, plodding and methodical, like a man who could not be defeated. That night he was too weary to build a fire, and too worried to eat the last of his food.

Next day Tappan was not unalive to the

changing character of the forest. He had worked down out of the zone of the spruce trees; the pines had thinned out and decreased in size; oak trees began to show prominently. All these signs meant that he was getting down out of the mountain heights. But the fact, hopeful as it was, had drawbacks. The snow was still four feet deep on a level and the crust held Tappan only about half the time. Moreover, the lay of the land operated against Tappan's progress. The long, slowly descending ridge had failed. There were no more canyons, but ravines and swales were numerous. Tappan dragged on, stern, indomitable, bent to his toil.

When the crust let him down, he hung his snowshoes over Jenet's back, and wallowed through, making a lane for her to follow. Two days of such heart-breaking toil, without food or fire, broke Tappan's magnificent endurance. But not his spirit! He hauled Jenet over the snow, and through the snow, down the hills and up the slopes, through the thickets, knowing that over the next ridge, perhaps, was deliverance. Deer and elk tracks began to be numerous. Cedar and juniper trees now predominated. An occasional pine showed here and there. He was getting out of the forest land. Only such mighty and justifiable hope as that could have kept him on his feet.

He fell often, and it grew harder to rise and go on. The hour came when the crust failed altogether to hold Tappan, and he had to abandon hauling Jenet. It was necessary to make a road for her. How weary, cold, horrible, the white reaches! Yard by yard Tappan made his way. He no longer sweat. He had no feeling in his feet or legs. Hunger ceased to gnaw at his vitals. His thirst he quenched with snow—soft snow now, that did not have to be crunched like ice. The pangs in his breast were terrible—cramps, constrictions, the piercing pains in his lungs, the dull ache of his overtaxed heart.

Tappan came to an opening in the cedar forest from which he could see afar. A long slope fronted him. It led down and down to open country. His desert eyes, keen as those of an eagle, made out flat country, sparsely covered with snow, and black dots that were cattle. The last slope! The last pull! Three feet of snow, except in drifts; down and down he plunged, making way for Jenet! All that day he toiled and fell and rolled down this league-long slope, wearing towards sunset to the end of his task, and likewise to the end of his will.

Now he seemed up and now down. There was no sense of cold or weariness. Only direction! Tappan still saw! The last of his horror at the monotony of white faded from his mind. Jenet was there, beginning to be able to travel for herself. The solemn close of endless day found Tappan arriving at the edge of the timbered country, where wind-bared patches of ground showed long, bleached grass. Jenet took to grazing.

As for Tappan, he fell with the tarpaulin, under a thick cedar, and with strengthless hands plucked and plucked at the canvas to spread it, so that he could cover himself. He looked again for Jenet. She was there, somehow a fading image, strangely blurred. She was grazing. Tappan lay down, and stretched out, and slowly drew the tarpaulin over him.

A piercing cold night wind swept down from the snowy heights. It wailed in the edge of the cedars and moaned out towards the open country. Yet the night seemed silent. The stars shone white in a deep blue sky— passionless, cold, watchful eyes, looking down without pity or hope or censure. They were the eyes of Nature. Winter had locked the heights in its snowy grip. All night that winter wind blew down, colder and colder. Then dawn broke, steely, gray, with a flare in the east.

Jenet came back where she had left her master. Camp! As she had returned thousands of dawns in the long years of her service. She had grazed all night. Her sides that had been flat were now full. Jenet had weathered another vicissitude of her life. She stood for a while, in a doze, with one long ear down over her meek face. Jenet was waiting for Tappan.

But he did not stir from under the long roll of canvas. Jenet waited. The winter sun rose in cold yellow flare. The snow glistened as with a crusting of diamonds. Somewhere in the distance sounded a long-drawn, discordant bray. Jenet's ears shot up. She listened. She recognized the call of one of her kind. Instinct always prompted Jenet. Sometimes she did bray. Lifting her gray head she sent forth a clarion: *"Hee-haw hee-haw-haw—hee-haw how-e-e-e!"*

That stentorian call started the echoes. They pealed down the slope and rolled out over the open country, clear as a bugle blast, yet hideous in their discordance. But this morning Tappan did not awaken.

CANYON WALLS

1

"WAL, HEAH'S ANOTHER FORKIN' OF THE TRAIL," said Monty, as he sat cross-legged on his saddle and surveyed the prospect. "Thet Mormon shepherd gave me a good steer. But doggone it, I hate to impose on anyone, even Mormons."

The scene was Utah, north of the great canyon, with the wild ruggedness and magnificence of that region visible on all sides. Monty could see clear to the Pink Cliffs that walled the ranches and ranges northward from this country of breaks. He had come up out of the abyss, across the desert between Mt. Trumbull and Hurricane Ledge, and he did not look back. Kanab must be thirty or forty miles, as a crow flies, across this valley dotted with sage. But Monty did not know Utah, or anything of this north rim country.

He rolled his last cigarette. He was hungry and worn out, and his horse was the same. Should he ride on to Kanab and throw in with one of the big cattle companies north of there, or should he take to one of the lonely canyons and hunt for a homesteader in need of a rider? The choice seemed hard to make, because Monty was tired of gun fights, of two-bit rustling, of gambling, and the other dubious means by which he had managed to live in Arizona. Not that Monty entertained any idea that he had ever reverted to real dishonesty! He had the free-range cowboy's elasticity of judgment. He could find excuses even for his latest escapade. But one or two more stunts like the one at Longhill would be bound to make him an outlaw. He reflected that if he were blamed for the Green Valley affair, also, which was not improbable, he might find himself already an outlaw, whether he personally agreed or not.

If he rode on to the north ranches, sooner or later someone from Arizona would come along; on the other hand, if he went down into the breaks of the canyon he might find a job and a hiding place where he would be safe until the whole thing blew over and was forgotten. Then he would take good care not to fall into another mess. Bad company and too free use of the bottle had brought Monty to this pass, which he really believed was completely undeserved.

Monty dropped his leg back and slipped his boot into the stirrup. He took the trail to the left and felt relief that the choice was made. It meant that he was avoiding towns and ranches, outfits of curious cowboys, and others who might have undue interest in wandering riders.

In about an hour, as the shepherd had directed, the trail showed up. It appeared to run along the rim of a canyon. Monty gazed down with approving eyes. The walls were steep and very deep, so deep that he could scarcely see the green squares of alfalfa, the orchards and pastures, the groves of cottonwoods, and a gray log cabin down below. He saw cattle and horses toward the upper end. At length the trail started down, and for a while thereafter Monty lost his perspective, and dismounting, he walked down the zigzag path leading his horse.

He saw, at length, that the canyon was boxed in by a wild notch of cliff and thicket and jumbled wall, from under which a fine stream of water flowed. There were still many acres that might have been under cultivation. Monty followed the trail along the brook, crossed it above where the floor of the canyon widened and the alfalfa fields lay richly green, and so on down a couple of miles to the cottonwoods. When he emerged from the fringe of trees, he was close to the cabin, and he could see where the canyon opened wide, with sheer red-gold walls, right out on the desert. It was sure enough a lonely retreat, far off the road, out of the grass country, a niche in the endless colored canyon walls.

The cottonwoods were shedding their fuzzy seeds that covered the ground like snow. An irrigation ditch ran musically through the yard. Chickens, turkeys, calves had the run of the place. The dry odor of the canyon here appeared to take on the fragrance of wood smoke and fresh baked bread.

Monty limped on, up to the cabin porch, which was spacious and comfortable, where no doubt the people who lived here spent many hours during fine weather. He saw a girl through the open door. She wore gray linsey, ragged and patched. His second glance made note of her superb build, her bare feet, her brown arms, and eyes that did not need half their piercing quality to see through Monty.

"Howdy, miss," hazarded Monty, though this was Mormon country.

"Howdy, stranger," she replied, very pleasantly, so that Monty decided to forget that he was looking for a fictitious dog.

"Could a thirsty rider get a drink around heah?"

"There's the brook. Best water in Utah."

"An' how about a bite to eat?"

"Tie up your horse and go around to the back porch."

Monty did as he was bidden, not without a few more glances at the girl, who he observed made no movement. But as he turned the corner of the house he heard her call, "Ma, there's a tramp gentile cowpoke coming back for a bite to eat."

When Monty reached the rear porch, another huge enclosure under the cottonwoods, he was quite prepared to encounter a large woman, of commanding presence, but of most genial and kindly face.

"Good afternoon, ma'am," began Monty, lifting his sombrero. "Shore you're the mother to thet gurl out in front—you look alike an' you're both orful handsome—but I won't be took fer no tramp gentile cowpuncher."

The woman greeted him with a pleasant laugh. "So, young man, you're a Mormon?"

"No, I ain't no Mormon, either. But particular, I ain't no tramp cowpoke," replied Monty with spirit, and just then the young person who had roused it appeared in the back doorway, with a slow, curious smile on her face. "I'm just lost an' tuckered out an' hungry."

For reply she motioned to a pan and bucket of water on a nearby bench, and a clean towel hanging on the rail. Monty was quick to take the hint, but performed his ablutions most deliberately. When he was ready at last, his face shining and refreshed, the woman was setting a table for him, and she bade him take a seat.

"Ma'am, I only asked fer a bite," he said.

"It's no matter. We've plenty."

And presently Monty sat down to a meal that surpassed any feast he had ever attended. It was his first experience at a Mormon table, the fame of which was known on every range. He had to admit that distance and exaggeration had not lent enchantment here. Without shame he ate until he could hold no more, and when he arose he made the Mormon mother a gallant bow.

"Lady, I never had sech a good dinner in all my life," he said fervently. "An' I reckon it won't make no difference if I never get another. Jest rememberin' this one will be enough."

"Blarney. You gentiles shore have the gift of gab. Set down and rest a little."

Monty was glad to comply, and leisurely disposed his long, lithe, dusty self in a comfortable chair. He laid his sombrero on the floor, and hitched his gun around, and looked up, genially aware that he was being taken in by two pairs of eyes.

"I met a shepherd lad on top an' he directed me to Andrew Boller's ranch. Is this heah the place?"

"No. Boller's is a few miles further on. It's the first big ranch over the Arizona line."

"Shore I missed it. Wal, it was lucky fer me. Are you near the Arizona line heah?"

"We're just over it."

"Oh, I see. Not in Utah atall," said Monty thoughtfully. "Any men about?"

"No. I'm the Widow Keetch, and this is my daughter Rebecca."

Monty guardedly acknowledged the introduction, without mentioning his own name, an omission the shrewd, kindly woman evidently noted. Monty was quick to feel that she must have had vast experience with menfolk. The girl, however, wore an indifferent, almost scornful air.

"This heah's a good-sized ranch. Must be a hundred acres jist in alfalfa," continued Monty. "You don't mean to tell me you two womenfolks run this ranch alone?"

"We do, mostly. We hire the plowing, and we have firewood hauled. And we always have a boy around. But year in and out we do most of the work ourselves."

"Wal, I'll be dogged!" exclaimed Monty. "Excuse me—but it shore is somethin' to heah. The ranch ain't so bad run down at thet. If you'll allow me to say so, Mrs. Keetch, it could be made a first-rate ranch. There's acres of uncleared land."

"My husband used to think so," replied the widow sighing. "But since he's gone we have just about managed to live."

"Wal, wal! Now I wonder what made me ride down the wrong trail. . . . Mrs. Keetch, I reckon you could use a fine, young, sober, honest, hard-workin' cowhand who knows all there is about ranchin'."

Monty addressed the woman in cool easy speech, quite deferentially, and then he shifted his gaze to the dubious face of the daughter. He was discovering that it had a compelling charm. She laughed outright, as if to say that she knew what a liar he was! That not only discomfited Monty, but roused his ire. The sassy Mormon filly!

"I guess I could use such a young man," returned Mrs. Keetch shortly, with her penetrating eyes on him.

"Wal, you're lookin' at him right now," said Monty fervently. "An' he's seein' nothin' less than the hand of Providence heah."

The woman stood up decisively. "Fetch your horse around," she said, and walked off the porch to wait for him. Monty made haste, his mind in a whirl. What was going to happen now? That girl! He ought to ride right on out of this canyon; and he was making up his mind to do it when he came back round the house to see that the girl had come to the porch rail. Her great eyes were looking at his horse. The stranger did not need to be told that she had a passion for horses. It would help some. But she did not appear to see Monty at all.

"You've a fine horse," said Mrs. Keetch. "Poor fellow! He's lame and tuckered out. We'll turn him loose in the pasture."

Monty followed her down a shady lane of cottonwoods, where the water ran noisily on each side, and he trembled inwardly at the content of the woman's last words. He had heard of the Good Samaritan ways of the Mormons. And in that short walk Monty did a deal of thinking. They reached an old barn beyond which lay a green pasture with an orchard running down one side. Peach trees were in bloom, lending a delicate border of pink to the fresh spring foliage.

"What wages would you work for?" asked the Mormon woman earnestly.

"Wal, come to think of thet, for my board an' keep. . . . Anyhow till we get the ranch payin'," replied Monty.

"Very well, stranger, that's a fair deal. Unsaddle your horse and stay," said the woman.

"Wait a minnit, ma'am," drawled Monty. "I got to substitute somethin' fer thet recommend I gave you. . . . Shore I know cattle an' ranchin' backward. But I reckon I should have said I'm a no-good, gun-throwin' cowpuncher who got run out of Arizona."

"What for?" demanded Mrs. Keetch.

"Wal, a lot of it was bad company an' bad licker. But at thet I wasn't so drunk I didn't know I was rustlin' cattle."

"Why do you tell me this?" she demanded.

"Wal, it is kinda funny. But I jist couldn't fool a kind woman like you. Thet's all."

"You don't look like a hard-drinking man."

"Aw, I'm not. I never said so, ma'am. Fact is, I ain't much of a drinkin' cowboy, atall."

"You came across the canyon?" she asked.

"Shore, an' by golly, thet was the orfullest ride, an' slide, an' swim, an' climb I ever had. I really deserve a heaven like this, ma'am."

"Any danger of a sheriff trailing you?"

"Wal, I've thought about thet. I reckon one chance in a thousand."

"He'd be the first one I ever heard of from across the canyon, at any rate. This is a lonesome, out-of-the-way place—and if you stayed away from the Mormon ranches and towns—"

"See heah, ma'am," interrupted Monty sharply. "You shore ain't goin' to take me on?"

"I am. You might be a welcome change. Lord knows I've hired every kind of a man. But not one of them ever lasted. You might."

"What was wrong with them hombres?"

"I don't know. I never saw much wrong except they neglected their work to moon around after Rebecca. But she could not get along with them, and she always drove them away."

"Aw, I see," exclaimed Monty, who did not see at all. "But I'm not one of the moonin' kind, ma'am, an' I'll stick."

"All right. It's only fair, though, to tell you there's a risk. The young fellow doesn't live who can seem to let Rebecca alone. If he could he'd be a godsend to a distracted old woman."

Monty wagged his bare head thoughtfully and slid the brim of his sombrero through his fingers. "Wal, I reckon I've been most everythin' but a gawdsend, an' I'd shore like to try thet."

"What's your name?" she asked with those searching gray eyes on him.

"Monty Bellew, Smoke fer short, an' it's shore shameful well known in some parts of Arizona."

"Any folks living?"

"Yes, back in Iowa. Father an' mother gettin' along in years now. An' a kid sister growed up."

"You send them money every month, of course?"

Monty hung his head. "Wal, fact is, not so reg'lar as I used to. . . . Late years times have been hard fer me."

"Hard nothing! You've drifted into hard ways. Shiftless, drinking, gambling, shooting cowhand—now, haven't you been just that?"

"I'm sorry, ma'am—I—I reckon I have."

"You ought to be ashamed. I know boys. I raised nine. It's time you were turning over a new leaf. Suppose we begin by burying that name Monty Bellew."

"I'm shore willin' an' grateful, ma'am."

"Then it's settled. Tend to your horse. You can have the little cabin there under the big cottonwood. We've kept that for our hired

help, but it hasn't been occupied much
lately."

She left Monty then and returned to the
ranch house. And he stood a moment irres-
olute. What a balance was struck there!
Presently he slipped saddle and bridle off the
horse, and turned him into the pasture.
"Baldy, look at thet alfalfa," he said. Weary
as Baldy was he lay down and rolled and
rolled.

Monty carried his equipment to the tiny
porch of the cabin under the huge cottonwood. He removed his saddlebags, which
contained the meager sum of his posses-
sions. Then he flopped down on a bench.

"Doggone it!" he muttered. His senses
seemed to be playing with him. The leaves
rustled above and the white cottonseeds
floated down; the bees were murmuring; water tinkled softly beyond the porch; somewhere a bell on a sheep or calf broke the
stillness. Monty had never felt such peace
and tranquillity, and his soul took on a burden of gratitude.

Suddenly a clear, resonant voice called out
from the house. "Ma, what's the name of our
new hand?"

"Ask him, Rebecca. I forgot to," replied the
mother.

"If that isn't like you!"

Monty was on his way to the house and
soon hove in sight of the young woman on
the porch. His heart thrilled as he saw her.

And he made himself some deep, wild promises.

"Hey, cowboy. What's your name?" she called.

"Sam," he called back.

"Sam what?"

"Sam Hill."

"For the land's sake! . . . That's not your name."

"Call me Land's Sake, if you like it better."

"*I* like it?" She nodded her curly head sagely, and she regarded Monty with a certainty that made him vow to upset her calculations or die in the attempt. She handed him down a bucket. "Can you milk a cow?"

"I never saw my equal as a milker," asserted Monty.

"In that case I won't have to help," she replied. "But I'll go with you to drive in the cows."

2

Fʀᴏᴍ ᴛʜᴀᴛ ʜᴏᴜʀ ᴅᴀᴛᴇᴅ Mᴏɴᴛʏ's ᴀᴘᴘᴀʀᴇɴᴛ subjection. He accepted himself at Rebecca's valuation—that of a very small hired boy. Monty believed he had a way with girls, but evidently that way had never been tried upon this imperious young Mormon miss.

Monty made good his boast about being a master hand at the milking of cows. He surprised Rebecca, though she did not guess that he was aware of it. For the rest, Monty never looked at her when she was looking, never addressed her, never gave her the slightest hint that he was even conscious of her sex.

Now he knew perfectly well that his appearance did not tally with this domesticated kind of a cowboy. She realized it and was puzzled, but evidently he was a novelty to her. At first Monty sensed the usual slight antagonism of the Mormon against the gentile, but in the case of Mrs. Keetch he never noticed this at all, and less and less from the girl.

The feeling of being in some sort of trance persisted with Monty, and he could not account for it, unless it was the charm of this lonely Canyon Walls Ranch, combined with the singular attraction of its young mistress. Monty had not been there three days before he realized that sooner or later he would fall, and great would be the fall thereof. But his sincere and ever-growing admiration for the Widow Keetch held him true to his promise. It would not hurt him to have a terrible case over Rebecca, and he resigned himself to his fate. Nothing could come of it, except perhaps to chasten him. Certainly he would never let her dream of such a thing. All the same, she just gradually and imperceptibly grew on Monty. There was nothing strange in this. Wherever Monty had ridden there had always been some girl who had done something to his heart. She might be a fright—a lanky, slab-sided, red-headed country girl—but that had made no difference. His comrades had called him Smoke Bellew, because of his propensity for raising so much smoke where there was not even any fire.

* * *

Sunday brought a change at the Keetch household. Rebecca appeared in a white dress and Monty caught his breath. He worshiped from a safe distance through the leaves. Presently a two-seated buckboard drove up to the ranch house, and Rebecca lost no time climbing in with the young people. They drove off, probably to church at the village of White Sage, some half dozen miles across the line. Monty thought it odd that Mrs. Keetch did not go.

There had been many a time in Monty's life when the loneliness and solitude of these dreaming canyon walls might have been maddening. But Monty found strange ease and solace here. He had entered upon a new era in his life. He hated to think that it might not last. But it would last if the shadow of the past did not fall on Canyon Walls.

At one o'clock Rebecca returned with her friends in the buckboard. And presently Monty was summoned to dinner, by no less than Mrs. Keetch's trenchant call. He had not anticipated this, but he brushed and brightened himself up a bit, and proceeded to the house. Mrs. Keetch met him as he mounted the porch steps. "Folks," she announced, "this is our new man, Sam Hill. . . . Sam, meet Lucy Card and her brother Joe, and Hal Stacey."

Monty bowed, and took the seat assigned to him by Mrs. Keetch. She was beaming, and the dinner table fairly groaned with the

load of good things to eat. Monty defeated
an overwhelming desire to look at Rebecca.
In a moment he saw that the embarrassment
under which he was laboring was silly. These
Mormon young people were quiet, friendly,
and far from curious. His presence at Widow
Keetch's table was more natural to them
than it seemed to him. Presently he was at
ease and dared to glance across the table.
Rebecca was radiant. How had it come that he
had not observed her beauty before? She appeared like a gorgeous opening rose. Monty
did not risk a second glance and he thought
that he ought to go far up the canyon and crawl
into a hole. Nevertheless, he enjoyed the dinner and did ample justice to it.

After dinner more company arrived, mostly
on horseback. Sunday was evidently the
Keetchs' day at home. Monty made several
unobtrusive attempts to escape, once being
stopped in his tracks by a single glance from
Rebecca, and the other times failing through
the widow's watchfulness. He felt that he
was very dense not to have noticed sooner
how they wished him to feel at home with
them. At length, toward evening, Monty left
Rebecca to several of her admirers, who out-
stayed the other visitors, and went off for a
sunset stroll under the canyon walls.

Monty did not consider himself exactly a
dunce, but he could not interpret clearly the
experience of the afternoon. There were,

however, some points that he could be sure of. The Widow Keetch had evidently seen better days. She did not cross the Arizona line into Utah. Rebecca was waited upon by a host of Mormons, to whom she appeared imperiously indifferent one moment and alluringly coy the next. She was a spoiled girl, Monty decided. He had not been able to discover the slightest curiosity or antagonism toward him in these visitors, and as they were all Mormons and he was a gentile, it changed some preconceived ideas of his.

Next morning the new hand plunged into the endless work that needed to be done about the ranch. He doubled the amount of water in the irrigation ditches, to Widow Keetch's delight. And that day passed as if by magic. It did not end, however, without Rebecca crossing Monty's trail, and it earned for him a very pleasant compliment from her, anent the fact that he might develop into a real good milkman.

The days flew by and another Sunday came, very like the first one, and that brought the month of June around. Thereafter the weeks were as short as days. Monty was amazed to see what a diversity of tasks he could put an efficient hand to. But, then, he had seen quite a good deal of ranch service in his time, aside from driving cattle. And it so happened that here was an ideal farm awaiting development, and he put his heart and soul into the task. The summer was hot, especially in the afternoon under the reflected heat from the canyon walls. He had cut alfalfa several times. And the harvest of fruit and grain was at hand. There were pumpkins so large that Monty could scarcely roll one over; bunches of grapes longer than his arm; great luscious peaches that shone like gold in the sunlight, and other farm products of proportionate size.

The womenfolk spent days putting up preserves, pickles, fruit. Monty used to go out of his way to smell the fragrant wood fire in the back yard under the cottonwoods, where the big brass kettle steamed with peach butter. "I'll shore eat myself to death when winter comes," he said.

Among the young men who paid court to Rebecca were two brothers, Wade and Eben Tyler, lean-faced, still-eyed young Mormons who were wild-horse hunters. The whole southern end of Utah was overrun by droves of wild horses, and according to some of the pioneers they were becoming a menace to the range. The Tylers took such a liking to Monty, the Keetchs' new hand, that they asked Mrs. Keetch to let him go with them on a hunt in October, over in what they called the Siwash. The widow was prevailed upon to give her consent, stipulating that Monty should fetch back a supply of venison. And Rebecca said she would allow him to go if he brought her one of the wild mustangs with a long mane and a tail that touched the ground.

So when October rolled around, Monty rode off with the brothers, and three days' riding brought them to the edge of a wooded region called the Buckskin Forest. It took a whole day to ride through the magnificent spruces and pines to reach the rim of the canyon. Here Monty found the wildest and most wonderful country he had ever seen. The Siwash was a rough section where the breaks in the rim afforded retreat for the thousands of deer and wild horses, as well as the cougars that preyed upon them. Monty had the hunt of his life, and by the time these fleeting weeks were over, he and the Tylers were fast friends.

Monty returned to Canyon Walls Ranch, pleased to find that he had been sorely needed and missed by the Keetches, and he was keen to have a go at his work again. Gradually he thought less and less of that Arizona escapade which had made him a fugitive. A little time spent in that wild country had a tendency to make past things appear dim and faraway. He ceased to start whenever he saw strange riders coming up the canyon gateway. Mormon sheepmen and cattlemen, when in the vicinity of Canyon Walls, always paid the Keetches a visit. Still Monty never ceased to pack a gun, a fact that Mrs. Keetch often mentioned. Monty said it was just a habit that he hadn't gotten over from his cattle-driving days.

He went to work clearing the upper end of the canyon. The cottonwood, scrub oak, and brush were as thick as a jungle. But day by day the tangle was mowed down under the sweep of Monty's ax. In his boyhood on the Iowa farm he had been a rail splitter. How many useful things were coming back to him! Every day Rebecca or Mrs. Keetch or the boy, Randy, who helped at chores, drove up in the big go-devil and hauled firewood. And when the winter's wood, with plenty to spare, had been stored away, Mrs. Keetch pointed with satisfaction to a considerable saving of money.

The leaves did not change color until late in November, and then they dropped reluctantly, as if not sure that winter could actually come to Canyon Walls this year. Monty even began to doubt that it would. But frosty mornings did come, and soon thin skims of ice formed on the still pools. Sometimes when he rode out of the canyon gateway on the desert, he could see the white line reaching down from the Buckskin, and Mt. Trumbull was wearing its crown of snow. But no real winter came to the canyon. The gleaming walls seemed to have absorbed enough of the summer sun to carry over. Every hour of daylight found Monty outdoors at one of the tasks which multiplied under his eye. After supper he would sit before the little stone fireplace he had built in his cabin, and watch the flames, and wonder about himself and how long this interlude could last. He began to wonder why it could not last always; and he went so far in his calculation as to say that a debt paid fully canceled even the acquiring of a few cattle not his own, in that past which receded ever farther over time's horizon. After all, he had been just a wild, irresponsible cowboy, urged on by drink and a need of money. At first he had asked only that it be forgotten and buried; but now he began to think he wanted to square that debt.

The winter passed, and Monty's labors had opened up almost as many new acres as had been cleared originally. Canyon Walls Ranch now took the eye of Andrew Boller, who made Widow Keetch a substantial offer for it. Mrs. Keetch laughed her refusal, and the remark she made to Boller mystified Monty for many a day. It was something about Canyon Walls someday being as great a ranch as that one of which the church had deprived her!

Monty asked Wade Tyler what the widow had meant, and Wade replied that he had once heard how John Keetch had owed the bishop a sum of money, and that the great ranch, after Keetch's death, had been confiscated. But that was one of the few questions Monty never asked Mrs. Keetch. The complexity and mystery of the Mormon Church did not interest him. It had been a shock, however, to find that two of Mrs. Keetch's Sunday callers, openly courting Rebecca's hand, already had wives. "By golly, I ought to marry her myself," declared Monty with heat, as he thought beside his fire, and then he laughed at his conceit. He was only Rebecca's hired help.

How good it was to see the green burst out again upon the cottonwoods, and the pink on the peach trees! Monty had now been at Canyon Walls a full year. It seemed incredible to him. It was the longest spell he had ever remained in one spot. He could see a vast change in the ranch. And what greater transformation had that labor wrought in him!

"Sam, we're going to need help this spring," said Mrs. Keetch one morning. "We'll want a couple of men and a teamster—a new wagon."

"Wal, we shore need aplenty," drawled Monty, "an' I reckon we'd better think hard."

"This ranch is overflowing with milk and honey. Sam, you've made it blossom. We must make some kind of a deal. I've wanted to speak to you before, but you always put me off. We ought to be partners."

"There ain't any hurry, ma'am," replied Monty. "I'm happy heah, an' powerful set on makin' the ranch a goin' concern. Funny no farmer heahabouts ever saw its possibilities afore. Wal, thet's our good luck."

"Boller wants my whole alfalfa cut this

year," continued Mrs. Keetch. "Saunders, a big cattleman, no Mormon by the way, is ranging south. And Boller wants to gobble all the feed. How much alfalfa will we be able to cut this year?"

"Countin' the new acreage, upward of two hundred tons."

"Sam Hill!" she cried incredulously.

"Wal, you needn't Sam Hill me. I get enough of thet from Rebecca. But you can gamble on the ranch from now on. We have the soil an' the sunshine—twice as much an' twice as hot as them farmers out in the open. An' we have water. Lady, we're goin' to grow things on the Canyon Wall."

"It's a dispensation of the Lord," she exclaimed fervently.

"Wal, I don't know about thet, but I can guarantee results. We start some new angles this spring. There's a side canyon up heah thet I cleared. Jist the place fer hogs. You know what a waste of fruit there was last fall. We'll not waste anythin' from now on. We can raise feed enough to pack this canyon solid with turkeys, chickens, an' hogs."

"Sam, you're a wizard, and the Lord surely guided me that day I took you on," replied Mrs. Keetch. "We're independent now and I see prosperity ahead. When Andrew Boller offered to buy this ranch I saw the handwriting on the wall."

"You bet. An' the ranch is worth twice what he offered."

"Sam, I've been an outcast too, in a way, but this will sweeten my cup."

"Wal, ma'am, you never made me no confidences, but I always took you fer the happiest woman I ever seen," declared Monty stoutly.

At this juncture Rebecca Keetch, who had been listening thoughtfully to the talk, as was her habit, spoke feelingly: "Ma, I want a lot of new dresses. I haven't a decent rag to my back. And look there!" She stuck out a shapely foot, bursting from an old shoe. "I want to go to Salt Lake City and buy some things. And if we're not poor any more—"

"My dear daughter, *I* cannot go to Salt Lake," interrupted the mother, a tone of sadness in her voice.

"But I can. Sue Tyler is going with her mother," burst out Rebecca eagerly. "Why can't I go with them?"

"Of course, daughter, you must have clothes to wear. And I have long thought of that. But to go to Salt Lake! . . . I don't know. It worries me. . . . Sam, what do you think of Rebecca's idea?"

"Which one?" asked Monty.

"About going to Salt Lake to buy clothes."

"Perfickly redic'lous," replied Monty blandly.

"*Why?*" flashed Rebecca, turning upon him with her great eyes aflame.

"Wal, you don't need no clothes in the fust place—"

"Don't I?" demanded Rebecca hotly. "You bet I don't need any clothes for *you*. You never even look at me. I could go around here positively stark naked and you'd never even see me."

"An' in the second place," continued Monty, with a wholly assumed imperturbability, "you're too young an' too crazy about boys to go on sech a long journey alone."

"Daughter, I—I think Sam is right," said Rebecca's mother.

"I'm eighteen years old," cried Rebecca. "And I wouldn't be going alone."

"Sam means you should have a man with you."

Rebecca stood for a moment in speechless rage, then she broke down. "Why doesn't the damn fool—offer to take me—then?"

"*Rebecca!*" cried Mrs. Keetch, horrified.

Monty meanwhile had been undergoing a remarkable transformation.

"Lady, if I was her dad—"

"But you're—not," sobbed Rebecca.

"Shore it's lucky fer you I'm not. For I'd spank some sense into you. . . . But I was goin' to say I'd drive you back from Kanab. You could go that far with the Tylers."

"There, daughter. . . . And maybe next year you *could* go to Salt Lake," added Mrs. Keetch consolingly.

Rebecca accepted the miserable compromise, but it was an acceptance she did not

106

care for, as was made plain to Monty by the dark look she gave him as she flounced away.

"Oh, dear," sighed Mrs. Keetch. "Rebecca is a good girl. But nowadays she often flares up like that. And lately she had been acting queer. If she'd only set her heart on some man!"

3

Monty had his doubts about the venture to which he had committed himself. But he undertook it willingly enough, because Mrs. Keetch was obviously so pleased and relieved. She evidently feared for this high-spirited girl. And so it turned out that Rebecca rode as far as Kanab with the Tylers, with the understanding that she would return in Monty's wagon.

The drive took Monty all day and there was a good deal of upgrade in the road. He did not believe he could make the thirty miles back in daylight hours, unless he got a very early start. And he just about knew he never could get Rebecca Keetch to leave Kanab before dawn. Still the whole prospect was one that offered adventure, and much of Monty's old devil-may-care spirit seemed roused to meet it.

He camped on the edge of town, and next morning drove in and left the old wagon at a blacksmith shop for needed repairs. The four horses were turned into pasture. Then Monty went about executing Mrs. Keetch's instructions, which had to do with engaging helpers and making numerous purchases. That evening saw a big, brand-new shiny wagon at the blacksmith shop, packed full of flour, grain, hardware, supplies, harness, and whatnot. The genial storekeeper who waited upon Monty averred that Mrs. Keetch must have had her inheritance returned to her. All the Mormons had taken a kindly interest in Monty and his work at Canyon Walls, which had become the talk all over the range. They were likable men, except for a few gray-whiskered old patriarchs who belonged to another day. Monty did not miss seeing several pretty Mormon girls; and their notice of him pleased him immensely, especially when Rebecca happened to be around to see.

Monty seemed to run into her every time he entered a store. She spent all the money she had saved up, and all her mother had given her, and she even borrowed the last few dollars he had in his pockets.

"Shore, you're welcome," said Monty in reply to her thanks. "But ain't you losin' your haid a little?"

"Well, so long's I don't lose it over *you,* what do you care?" she retorted, saucily, with another of those dark glances which had mystified him before.

Monty replied that her mother had expressly forbidden her to go into debt for anything.

"Don't you try to boss me, Sam Hill," she warned, but she was still too happy to be really angry.

"Rebecca, I don't care two bits what you do," said Monty shortly.

"Oh, don't you?— Thanks! You're always flattering me," she returned mockingly.

It struck Monty then that she knew something about him or about herself which he did not share.

"We'll be leavin' before sunup," he added briefly. "You'd better let me have all your bundles so I can take them out to the wagon an' pack them tonight."

Rebecca demurred, but would not give a reason, which could only have been because she wanted to gloat over her purchases. Monty finally prevailed upon her; and it took two trips for him and a boy he had hired to carry the stuff out to the blacksmith's shop.

"Lord, if it should rain!" said Monty, remembering that he had no extra tarpaulin. So he went back to the store and got one, and hid it, with the idea of having fun with Rebecca in case a storm threatened on the way back to the ranch.

After supper Rebecca drove out to Monty's camp with some friends.

"I don't care for your camping out like this. You should have gone to the inn," she said loftily.

"Wal, I'm used to campin'," he drawled.

"Sam, they're giving a dance for me tonight," announced Rebecca.

"Fine. Then you needn't go to bed atall, an' we can get an early start."

The young people with Rebecca shouted with laughter, and she looked dubious.

"Can't we stay over another day?"

"I should smile we cain't," retorted Monty with unusual force. "An' if we don't get an early start we'll never reach home tomorrow. So you jist come along heah, young lady, about four o'clock."

"In the morning?"

"In the mawnin'. I'll have some breakfast fer you."

It was noticeable that Rebecca made no rash promises. Monty rather wanted to give in to her—she was so happy and gay—but he remembered his obligations to Mrs. Keetch, and remained firm.

As they drove off Monty's sharp ears caught Rebecca complaining—"and I can't do a solitary thing with that stubborn Arizona cowpuncher."

This rather pleased Monty, as it gave him distinction, and was proof that he had not yet betrayed himself to Rebecca. He would proceed on these lines.

That night he did a remarkable thing, for him. He found out where the dance was being held, and peered through a window to see Rebecca in all her glory. He did not miss, however, the fact that she did not appear to outshine several other young women there. Monty stifled a yearning that had not bothered him for a long time. "Doggone it! I ain't no old gaffer. I could dance the socks off some of them Mormons." He became aware presently that between dances some of the young Mormon men came outdoors and indulged in desultory fist fights. He could not see any real reason for these encounters, and it amused him. "Gosh, I wonder if thet is jist a habit with these hombres. Fact is, though, there's shore not enough girls to go round. . . . Holy mackerel, how I'd like to have my old dancin' pards heah! Wouldn't we wade through thet corral! . . . I wonder what's become of Slim an' Cuppy, an' if they ever think of me. Doggone!"

Monty sighed and returned to camp. He was up before daylight, but did not appear to be in any rush. He had a premonition what to expect. Day broke and the sun tipped the low desert in the east, while Monty leisurely got breakfast. He kept an eye on the lookout for Rebecca. The new boy, Jake, arrived with shiny face, and later one of the men engaged by Mrs. Keetch came. Monty had the two teams fetched in from pasture, and hitched up. It was just as well that he had to wait for Rebecca, because the new harness did not fit and required skilled adjustment, but he was not going to tell her that. The longer she made him wait the longer would be the scolding she would get.

About nine o'clock she arrived in a very much overloaded buckboard. She was gay of attire and face, and so happy that Monty, had he been sincere with himself, could never have reproved her. But he did it, very sharply, and made her look like a chidden child before her friends. This reacted upon Monty so pleasurably that he began afresh. But this was a mistake.

"Yah! Yah! Yah!" she cried. And her friends let out a roar of merriment.

"Becky, you shore have a tiptop chaperon," remarked one frank-faced Mormon boy. And other remarks were not wanting to convey the hint that at least one young rider in the world had not succumbed to Rebecca's charms.

"Where am I going to ride?" she asked curtly.

Monty indicated the high driver's seat. "Onless you'd rather ride with them two new hands in the old wagon."

Rebecca scorned to argue with Monty, but climbed quickly to the lofty perch.

"Girls, it's nearer heaven than I've ever been yet," she called gayly.

"Just what do you mean, Becky?" replied a pretty girl with roguish eyes. "So high up— or because—"

"Go along with you," interrupted Rebecca with a blush. "You think of nothing but men. I wish you had . . . but good-by—good-by. I've had a lovely time."

Monty clambered to the driver's seat, and followed the other wagon out of town, down into the desert. Rebecca appeared to want to talk.

"Oh, it was a wonderful change! I had a grand time. But I'm glad you wouldn't let me go to Salt Lake. It'd have ruined me, Sam."

Monty felt subtly flattered, but he chose to remain aloof and disapproving.

"Nope. Hardly that. You was ruined long ago, Miss Rebecca," he drawled.

"Don't call me miss," she flashed. "And see here, Sam Hill—do you hate us Mormons?"

"I shore don't. I like all the Mormons I've met. They're jist fine. An' your ma is the best woman I ever knew."

"Then I'm the only Mormon you've no use for," she retorted with bitterness. "Don't deny it. I'd rather you didn't add falsehood to your—your other faults. It's a pity, though, that we can't get along. Mother depends on you now. You've certainly pulled us out of a hole. And I—I'd like you—if you'd let me. But you always make me out a wicked, spoiled girl. Which I'm not. . . . Why couldn't you come to the dance last night?

They wanted you. Those girls were eager to meet you."

"I wasn't asked—not thet I'd of come anyhow," stammered Monty.

"You know perfectly well that in a Mormon town or home you are always welcome," she said. "What did you want? Would you have had me stick my finger in the top hole of your vest and look up at you like a dying duck and say, 'Sam, please come'?"

"My Gawd, no. I never dreamed of wantin' you to do anythin'," replied Monty hurriedly. He was getting beyond his depth here, and began to doubt his ability to say the right things.

"*Why* not? Am I so hideous? Aren't I a human being? A *girl?*" she asked with resentful fire.

Monty deliberated a moment, as much to recover his scattered wits as to make an adequate reply.

"Wal, you shore are a live human critter. An' as handsome as any gurl I ever seen. But you're spoiled somethin' turrible. You're the most orful flirt I ever watched, an' the way you treat these fine Mormon boys is shore scandalous. You don't know what you want more'n one minnit straight runnin'. An' when you get what you want you're sick of it right away."

"Oh, is that *all?*" she burst out, and then followed with a peal of riotous laughter. But she did not look at him or speak to him again for several long hours.

Monty liked the silence better. He still had the thrill of her presence, without her disturbing chatter. A nucleus of a thought tried to wedge its way into his consciousness—that this girl was not completely indifferent to him. But he squelched it.

At noon they halted in a rocky depression, where water filled the holes, and Rebecca got down to sit in the shade of a cedar.

"I want something to eat," she declared imperiously.

"Sorry, but there ain't nothin'," replied Monty imperturbably, as he mounted to the seat again. The other wagon rolled on, crushing the rocks with its wide tires.

"Are you going to starve me into submission?"

Monty laughed at her. "Wal, I reckon if someone took a willow switch to your bare legs an'—wal, he might get a little submission out of you."

"You're worse than a Mormon," she cried in disgust, as if that was the very depth of depravity.

"Come along, youngster," said Monty with pretended weariness. "If we don't keep steppin' along lively we'll never get home tonight."

"Good! I'll delay you as much as I can. . . . Sam, I'm scared to death to face Mother." And she giggled.

"What about?"

"I went terribly in debt. But I didn't lose my 'haid' as you say. I thought it all out. I won't be going again for ages. And I'll work. It was the change in our fortunes that tempted me."

"Wal, I reckon we can get around tellin' your ma," said Monty lamely.

"You wouldn't give me away, Sam?" she asked in surprise, with strange intent eyes. And she got up to come over to the wagon.

"No, I wouldn't. Course not. What's more I can lend you the money—presently."

"Thanks, Sam. But I'll tell Mother."

She scrambled up and rode beside him again for miles without speaking. It seemed nothing to Monty to ride in that country and keep silent. The desert was not conducive to conversation. It was so beautiful that talking seemed out of place. Mile after mile of rock and sage, of black ridge and red swale, and always the great landmarks looming as if unattainable. Behind them the Pink Cliffs rose higher the farther they traveled; to their left the long black fringe of the Buckskin gradually sank into obscurity; in front rolled away the colorful desert, an ever-widening bowl that led the gaze to the purple chaos in the distance—that wild region of the riven earth called the canyon country.

Monty did not tell Rebecca that they could not get even half way home that day, and that they would have to make camp for the night.

But eventually, as a snow squall formed over Buckskin, he told her it likely would catch up with them and turn to rain.

"Oh, Sam!" she wailed. "If my things get wet!"

He did not give her any assurance or comfort, and about mid-afternoon, when the road climbed toward a low divide, he saw that they would not miss the storm. But he would make camp at the pines where they could easily weather it.

Before sunset they reached the highest point along the road, from which the spectacle down toward the west made Monty acknowledge that he was gazing at the grandest panorama his enraptured eyes had ever viewed.

Rebecca watched with him, and he could feel her absorption. Finally she sighed and said, as if to herself, "One reason I'll marry a Mormon—if I have to—is that I never want to leave Utah."

They halted in the pines, low down on the far side of the divide, where a brook brawled merrily, and here the storm, half snow and half rain, caught them. Rebecca was frantic. She did not know where her treasures were packed.

"Oh, Sam, I'll never forgive you!"

"*Me?* What have I got to do about it?" he asked, in pretended astonishment.

"Oh, you *knew* all the time that it would rain," she wailed. "And if you'd been half a man—if you didn't *hate* me so, you—you could have saved my things."

"Wal, if thet's how you feel about it I'll see what I can do," he drawled.

And in a twinkling he jerked out the tarpaulin and spread it over the new wagon where he had carefully packed her cherished belongings. And in the same twinkling her woebegone face changed to joy. Monty thought for a moment that she was going to kiss him and he was scared stiff.

"Ma was right, Sam. You are the wonderfullest man," she said. "But—why didn't you *tell* me?"

"I forgot, I reckon. Now this rain ain't goin' to amount to much. After dark it'll turn off cold. I put some hay in the bottom of the wagon, heah, an' a blanket. So you can sleep comfortable."

"*Sleep!* ... Sam, you're not going to stop here?"

"Shore am. This new wagon is stiff, an' the other one's heavy loaded. We're blamed lucky to reach this good campin' spot."

"But, Sam, we can't stay here. We must drive on. It doesn't make any difference how *long* we are, so that we keep moving."

"An' kill our horses, an' then not get in. Sorry, Rebecca. If you hadn't delayed us five hours we might have done it, allowin' fer faster travel in the cool of the mawnin'."

"Sam, do you want to see my reputation

119

ruined?" she asked, her great accusing eyes on him.

"Wal! . . . Rebecca Keetch, if you don't beat me! I'll tell you what, miss. Where I come from a man can entertain honest desire to spank a crazy gurl without havin' evil intentions charged agin him!"

"You can spank me to your heart's content—but—Sam—take me home first."

"Nope. I can fix it with your ma, an' I cain't see thet it amounts to a darn otherwise."

"Any Mormon girl who stayed out on the desert—all night with a gentile—would be ruined!" she declared.

"But we're not alone," yelled Monty, red in the face. "We've got two men and a boy with us."

"No Mormon will ever—believe it," sobbed Rebecca.

"Wal, then, to hell with the Mormons who won't," exclaimed Monty, exasperated beyond endurance.

"Mother will make you marry me," ended Rebecca, with such tragedy of eye and voice that Monty could not but believe such a fate would be worse than death for her.

"Aw, don't distress yourself Miss Keetch," responded Monty with profound dignity. "I couldn't be druv to marry you—not to save your blasted Mormon Church—nor the whole damn world of gentiles from—from conflaggeration!"

4

Next day Monty drove through White Sage at noon, and reached Canyon Walls about mid-afternoon, completing a journey he would not want to undertake again, under like circumstances. He made haste to unburden himself to his beaming employer.

"Wal, Mrs. Keetch, I done about everythin' as you wanted," he said. "But I couldn't get an early start yestiddy mawnin' an' so we had to camp at the pines."

"Why couldn't you?" she demanded, as if seriously concerned.

"Wal, fer several reasons, particular thet the new harness wouldn't fit."

"You shouldn't have kept Rebecca out all night," said the widow severely.

"I don't know how it could have been avoided," replied Monty mildly. "You wouldn't have had me kill four good horses."

"Did you meet anyone?" she asked.

"Not even a sheepherder."

"Did you stop at White Sage?"

"Only to water, an' we didn't see no one."

"Maybe we can keep the Mormons from finding out," returned Mrs. Keetch with relief. "I'll talk to these new hands. Mormons are close-mouthed when it's to their interest."

"Wal, ma'am, heah's the receipts, an' my notes an' expenditures," added Monty, handing them over. "My pore haid shore buzzed over all them figgers. But I got the prices you wanted. I found out you gotta stick to a Mormon. But he won't let you buy from no other storekeeper, if he can help it."

"Indeed he won't. . . . Well, daughter, what have you to say for yourself? I expected to see you with the happiest of faces. But you look the way you used to when you stole jam. I hope it wasn't your fault Sam had to keep you all night on the desert."

"Yes, Ma, it was," admitted Rebecca, and though she spoke frankly she plainly feared her mother's displeasure.

"So. And Sam wouldn't tell on you, eh?"

"No, I don't know why he wouldn't! Not out of any feelings for me. . . . Come in, Ma, and let me confess the rest—while I've still got the courage."

Mrs. Keetch looked worried. Monty saw that her anger would be a terrible thing if aroused.

"Ma'am, don't be hard on the gurl," he said, with his easy drawl and smile. "Jist think! She hadn't been to Kanab fer two years. Two years! An' she a growin' gurl. Kanab is some shucks of a town. I was surprised. An' she was jist a kid let loose."

"Sam Hill! So you have fallen into the ranks at last," exclaimed Mrs. Keetch, while Rebecca telegraphed him a grateful glance.

"Lady, I don't savvy about the ranks," replied Monty stiffly. "But I've been falling from grace all my life. Thet's why I'm—"

"No matter," interrupted the widow hastily, and it struck Monty that she did not care to have him confess his shortcomings before Rebecca. "Unpack the wagons and put the things on the porch, except what should go to the barn."

Monty helped the two new employees unpack the old wagon first, and then directed them to the barn. Then he removed Rebecca's many purchases and piled them on the porch. All the time his ears burned over the heated argument going on within the house. Rebecca seemed to have relapsed into tears while her mother still continued to upbraid her. Monty drove out to the barn considerably disturbed by the sound of the girl's uncontrolled sobbing.

"Doggone! The old lady's hell when she's

riled," he thought. "Now I wonder which it was. Rebecca spendin' all her money an' mine, an' this runnin' up bills—or because she made us stay a night out ... or mebbe it's somethin' I don't know a blamed thing about.... Whew, but she laid it onto thet pore kid. Doggone the old Mormon! She'd better not pitch into me."

Supper was late that night and the table was set in the dusk. Mrs. Keetch had regained her composure, but Rebecca's face was woebegone and pallid from weeping. Monty's embarrassment seemed augmented by the fact that she squeezed his hand under the table. But it was a silent meal, soon finished; and while Rebecca reset the table for the new employees, Mrs. Keetch drew Monty aside on the porch. It suited him just as well that dusk was deepening into night.

"I am pleased with the way you carried out my instructions," said Mrs. Keetch. "I could not have done so well. My husband John was never any good in business. You are shrewd, clever, and reliable. If this year's harvest shows anything near what you claim, I can do no less than make you my partner. There is nothing to prevent us from developing another canyon ranch. John had a lien on one west of here. It's bigger than this and uncleared. We could acquire that, if you thought it wise. In fact we could go far. Not that I am money mad, like many Mormons are. But I would like to show them. . . . What do you think about it, Sam?"

"Wal, I agree, 'cept makin' me full pardner seems more'n I deserve. But if the crops turn out big this fall—an' you can gamble on it— I'll make a deal with you fer five years or ten or life."

"Thank you. That is well. It insures comfort in my old age as well as something substantial for my daughter. . . . Sam, do you understand Rebecca?"

"Good Lord, no," exploded Monty.

"I reckoned you didn't. Do you realize that where she is concerned you are wholly unreliable?"

"What do you mean, ma'am?" he asked, thunderstruck.

"She can wind you round her little finger."

"Huh! . . . She jist cain't do anythin' of the sort," declared Monty, trying to appear angry. The old lady might ask a question presently that would be exceedingly hard to answer.

"Perhaps you do not know it. That'd be natural. At first I thought you a pretty deep, clever cowboy, one of the devil-with-the-girls kind, and that you would give Rebecca the lesson she deserves. But now I think you a soft-hearted, easy-going, *good* young man, actually stupid when it comes to a girl."

"Aw, thanks, ma'am," replied Monty, most uncomfortable, and then his natural spirit rebelled. "I never was accounted stupid about gentile gurls."

"Rebecca is no different from any girl. I should think you'd have seen that the Mormon style of courtship makes her sick. It is too simple, too courteous, too respectful, and too much bordering on the religious to stir her heart. No Mormon will ever get Rebecca, unless I force her to marry him. Which I have been pressed to do and which I hope I shall never do."

"Wal, I respect you fer thet, ma'am," replied Monty feelingly. "But why all this talk about Rebecca? I'm shore mighty sympathetic, but how does it concern me?"

"Sam, I have not a friend in all this land, unless it's you."

"Wal, you can shore gamble on me. If you want I—I'll marry you an' be a dad to this gurl who worries you so."

"Bless your heart! . . . No, I'm too old for that, and I would not see you sacrifice yourself. But, oh, wouldn't that be fun—and revenge?"

"Wal, it'd be heaps of fun," laughed Monty. "But I don't reckon where the revenge would come in."

"Sam, you've given me an idea," spoke up the widow, in a quick whisper. "I'll threaten Rebecca with this. That I could marry you and make you her father. If that doesn't chasten her—then the Lord have mercy upon us."

"She'd laugh at you."

"Yes. But she'll be scared to death. I'll never forget her face one day when she confessed that you claimed she should be switched—well, it must have been sort of shocking, if you said it."

"I shore did, ma'am," he admitted.

"Well, we begin all over again from today," concluded the widow thoughtfully. "To build anew! Go back to your work and plans. I have the utmost confidence in you. My troubles are easing. But I have not one more word of advice about Rebecca."

"I cain't say as you gave me any advice at all. But mebbe thet's because I'm stupid. Thanks, Mrs. Keetch, an' good night."

The painful hour of confused thinking which Monty put in that night, walking in the moonlight shadows under the canyon walls, resulted only in increasing his bewilderment. He ended it by admitting he was now in love with Rebecca, ten thousand times worse than he had ever loved any girl before, and that she could wind him around her little finger all she wanted to. If she knew! But he swore he would never let her find it out.

Next day seemed to bring the inauguration of a new regime at Canyon Walls. The ranch had received an impetus, like that given by water run over rich dry ground. Monty's hours were doubly full. Always there was

Rebecca, singing on the porch at dusk. "In the gloaming, oh my darling," a song that carried Monty back to home in Iowa, and the zigzag rail fences; or she was at his elbow during the milking hour, an ever-growing task; or in the fields. She could work, that girl; and he told her mother it would not take long for her to earn the money she had squandered in town.

Sunday after Sunday passed, with the usual host of merry callers, and no word was ever spoken of Rebecca having passed a night on the desert with a gentile. So that specter died, except in an occasional mocking look she gave him, which he took to mean that she still could betray herself and him if she took the notion.

In June came the first cutting of alfalfa—fifty acres with an enormous yield. The rich, green, fragrant hay stood knee high. Monty tried to contain himself. But it did seem marvelous that the few simple changes he had made could produce such a rich harvest.

Monty worked late, and a second bell did not deter him. He wanted to finish this last great stack of alfalfa. Then he saw Rebecca running along the trail, calling. Monty let her call. It somehow tickled him, pretending not to hear. So she came out into the field and up to him.

"Sam, are you deaf? Ma rang twice. And then she sent me."

"Wal, I reckon I been feelin' orful good about this alfalfa," he replied.

"Oh, it is lovely. So dark and green—so sweet to smell! . . . Sam, I'll just have to slide down that haystack."

"Don't you dare," called Monty in alarm.

But she ran around to the lower side and presently appeared on top, her face flushed, full of fun and the desire to torment him.

"Please, Rebecca, don't slide down. You'll topple it over, an' I'll have all the work to do over again."

"Sam, I just have to, the way I used to when I was a kid."

"You're a kid right now," he retorted. "An' go back an' get down careful."

She shrieked and let herself go and came sliding down, somewhat at the expense of modesty. Monty knew he was angry, but he feared that he was some other things too.

"There! You see how slick I did it? I could always beat the girls—and boys, too."

"Wal, let thet do," growled Monty.

"Just one more, Sam."

He dropped his pitchfork and made a lunge for her, catching only the air. How quick she was! He controlled an impulse to run after her. Soon she appeared on top again, with something added to her glee.

"Rebecca, if you slide down heah again you'll be sorry," he shouted warningly.

"What'll *you* do?"

"I'll spank you."

"Sam Hill . . . You wouldn't dare."

"So help me heaven, I will."

She did not in the least believe him, but it was evident that his threat made her project only the more thrilling. There was at least a possibility of excitement.

"Look out. I'm acoming," she cried, with a wild, sweet trill of laughter.

As she slid down Monty leaped to intercept her. A scream escaped from Rebecca, but it was only because of her unruly skirts. That did not deter Monty. He caught her and stopped her high off the ground, and there he pinioned her.

Whatever Monty's intent had been it now escaped him. A winged flame flicked at every fiber of his being. He had her arms spread, and it took all his strength and weight to hold her there, feet off the ground. She was not in the least frightened at this close contact, though a wonderful look of speculation sparkled in her big gray eyes.

"You caught me. Now what?" she said challengingly.

Monty kissed her square on the mouth.

"Oh!" she cried, obviously startled. Then a wave of scarlet rushed up from the rich gold swell of her neck to her forehead. She struggled. "Let me down—you—you gentile cowpuncher!"

Monty kissed her again, longer, harder than before. Then when she tried to scream he stopped her lips again.

"You—little Mormon—devil!" he panted. "This heah—was shore—comin' to you!"

"I'll kill you!"

"Wal, it'll be worth—dyin' fer, I reckon." Then Monty kissed her again and again until she gasped for breath, and when she sagged limp and unresisting into his arms he kissed her cheeks, her eyes, her hair, and like a madman whose hunger had been augmented by what it fed on he went back to her red parted lips.

Suddenly the evening sky appeared to grow dark. A weight carried him down with the girl. The top of the alfalfa stack had slid down upon them. Monty floundered out and dragged Rebecca from under the fragrant mass of hay. She did not move. Her eyes were closed. With trembling hand he brushed the chaff and bits of alfalfa off her white face. But her hair was full of them.

"My Gawd, I've played hob now," he whispered, as the enormity of his offense suddenly dawned upon him. Nevertheless, he felt a tremendous thrill of joy as he looked down at her. Only her lips bore a vestige of color. Suddenly her eyes opened wide. From the sheer glory of them Monty fled.

5

His first wild impulse, as he ran, was to get out of the canyon, away from the incomprehensible forces that had worked such sudden havoc with his life. His second thought was to rush to Mrs. Keetch and confess everything to her, before Rebecca could damn him forever in that good woman's estimation. Then by the time he had reached his cabin and thrown himself on the porch bench, both of these impulses had given place to still others. But it was not Monty's nature to remain helpless for long. Presently he sat up, wringing wet with sweat, and still shaking.

"Aw, what could have come over me?" he

breathed hoarsely. And suddenly he realized that nothing so terrible had happened after all. He had been furious with Rebecca and meant to chastise her. But when he held her close and tight, with those challenging eyes and lips right before him, all else except the sweetness of momentary possession had been forgotten. He loved the girl and had not before felt any realization of the full magnitude of his love. He believed that he could explain to Mrs. Keetch, so that she would not drive him away. But of course he would be as dirt under Rebecca's feet from that hour on. Yet even in his mournful acceptance of this fate his spirit rose in wonderment over what this surprising Mormon girl must be thinking of him now.

Darkness had almost set in. Down the lane Monty saw a figure approaching, quite some distance away, and he thought he heard a low voice singing. It could not be Rebecca. Rebecca would be weeping.

"RE-BECCA," called Mrs. Keetch from the porch, in her mellow, far-reaching voice.

"Coming, Ma," replied the girl.

Monty sank into the shadow of his little cabin. He felt small enough to be unseen, but dared not risk it. And he watched in fear and trepidation. Suddenly Rebecca's low contralto voice rang on the quiet sultry air.

In the gloaming, Oh my darling!
When the lights are dim and low—

133

And the quiet shadows falling,
Softly come and softly go.

Monty's heart swelled almost to bursting. Did she realize the truth and was she mocking him? He was simply flabbergasted. But how the sweet voice filled the canyon and came back in echo from the walls!

Rebecca, entering the square between the orchards and the cottonwoods, gave Monty's cabin a wide berth.

"Isn't Sam with you?" called Mrs. Keetch from the porch.

"Sam? . . . No, he isn't."

"Where is he? Didn't you call him? Supper is getting cold."

"I haven't any idea where Sam is. Last I saw of him he was running like mad," rejoined Rebecca with a giggle.

That giggle saved Monty from a stroke of apoplexy.

"Running? What for?" asked the mother, as Rebecca mounted the porch.

"Ma, it was the funniest thing. I called Sam, but he didn't hear. I went out to tell him supper was ready. He had a great high stack of alfalfa up. Of course I wanted to climb it and slide down. Well, Sam got mad and ordered me not to do any such thing. Then I *had* to do it. Such fun! Sam growled like a bear. Well, I couldn't resist climbing up for another slide. . . . Do you know, Mother, Sam got perfectly furious. He has a terrible temper. He commanded me not to slide off that stack. And when I asked him what he'd do if I did—he declared he'd spank me. Imagine! I only meant to tease him. I wasn't going to slide at all. Then, you can see I *had* to.... So I did.... I—oh dear!—I fetched the whole top of the stack down on us—and when I got out from under the smothering hay—and could see—there was Sam running for dear life."

"Well, for the land's sake!" exclaimed Mrs. Keetch dubiously, and then she laughed. "You drive the poor fellow wild with your pranks. Rebecca, will you never grow up?"

Whereupon she came out to the porch rail and called, "Sam."

Monty started up, opened his door to let it slam and replied, in what he thought a perfectly normal voice, "Hello?"

"Hurry to supper."

Monty washed his face and hands, brushed his hair, while his mind whirled. Then he sat down bewildered. "Doggone me!—Can you beat thet gurl? She didn't give me away—she didn't lie, yet she never tole.... She's not goin' to tell.... Must have been funny to her.... But shore it's a daid safe bet she never got kissed thet way before.... I jist cain't figger her out."

Presently he went to supper and was grateful for the dim light. Still he felt the girl's eyes on him. No doubt she was now appreciating him at last as a real Arizona cowboy. He pretended weariness, and soon hurried away to his cabin, where he spent a night of wakefulness and of conflicting emotions. Remorse, however, had died a natural death after hearing Rebecca's story to her mother.

With dawn came the blessed work into which Monty plunged, finding relief in tasks which kept him away from the ranch house.

For two whole weeks Rebecca did not speak a single word to him. Mrs. Keetch finally noticed the strange silence and reproved her daughter for her attitude.

"Speak to *him?*" asked Rebecca, with a sniff. "Maybe—when he crawls on his knees!"

"But, daughter, he only threatened to spank you. And I'm sure you gave him provocation. You must always forgive. We cannot live at enmity here," she said. "Sam is a good man, and we owe him much."

Then she turned to Monty.

"Sam, you know Rebecca had passed eighteen and she feels an exaggerated sense of her maturity. Perhaps if you'd tell her you were sorry—"

"What about?" asked Monty, when she hesitated.

"Why, about what offended Rebecca."

"Aw, shore. I'm orful sorry," drawled Monty, his keen eyes on the girl. "Turrible sorry—but it's about not sayin' an' doin' *more*—an' then spankin' her to boot."

Mrs. Keetch looked aghast, and when Re-

136

becca ran away from the table hysterical with mirth, the good woman seemed positively nonplused.

"That girl! Why, Sam, I thought she was furious with you. But she's not. It's all sham."

"Wal, I reckon she's riled all right, but it doesn't matter. An' see heah, ma'am," he went on, lowering his voice. "I'm confidin' in you, an' if you give me away—wal, I'll leave the ranch. . . . I reckon you've forgot how once you told me I'd lose my haid over Rebecca. Wal, I've lost it, clean an' plumb an' otherwise. An' sometimes I do queer things. Jist remember thet's why. This won't make no difference. I'm happy heah. Only I want you to understand me."

"Sam Hill!" she whispered in amazement. "So that's what ails you. . . . Now all will be well."

"Wal, I'm glad you think so," replied Monty shortly. "An' I reckon it will be—when I get over these growin' pains."

She leaned toward him. "My son, I understand now. Rebecca has been in love with you for a long time. Just let her alone. All will be well."

Monty gave her one mute, incredulous stare and then he fled. In the darkness of his cabin he persuaded himself of the absurdity of the sentimental Mrs. Keetch's claim. That night he could sleep. But when day came again he found that the havoc had been wrought. He found himself living in a kind of dream, and he was always watching for Rebecca.

Straightway he began to make some discoveries. Gradually she appeared to come out of her icy shell. She worked as usual, and apparently with less discontent, especially in the mornings when she had time to sew on the porch. She would fetch lunch to the men out in the fields. Once or twice Monty saw her on top of a haystack, but he always quickly looked away. She climbed the wall trail; she gathered armloads of wild flowers; she helped where her help was not needed.

On Sunday mornings she went to church at White Sage and in the afternoon entertained callers. But it was noticeable that her Mormon courters grew fewer as the summer advanced. Monty missed in her the gay allure, the open coquetry, the challenge that had once been so marked.

All this was thought-provoking enough for Monty, but nothing to the discovery that Rebecca watched him from afar and from near at hand. Monty could scarcely believe it. Only more proof of his addled brain! However, the eyes which had made Monty Smoke Bellew a great shot and tracker, wonderful out on the range, could not be deceived. When he himself took to spying upon Rebecca, he had learned the staggering truth.

In the mornings and evenings while he was at work near the barn or resting on his porch she watched him, believing herself unseen.

She peered from behind her window curtain, through the leaves, above her sewing, from the open doors—from everywhere her great gray hungry eyes sought him. It began to get on Monty's nerves. Did she hate him so much that she was planning some dire revenge? But the eyes that watched him in secret seldom or never met his own any more. Sometimes he would recall Mrs. Keetch's strangely tranquil words, and then he would have to battle fiercely with himself to recover his equanimity. The last asinine thing Smoke Bellew would ever do would be to believe that Rebecca loved him.

One noonday Monty returned to his cabin to find a magical change in his single room. He could not recognize it. Clean and tidy and colorful, it met his eye as he entered. There were Indian rugs on the clay floor, Indian ornaments on the log walls, curtains at his windows, a scarf on his table, and a bright bedspread on his bed. In a little Indian vase on the table stood some stalks of golden daisies and purple asters.

"What happened around heah this mawnin'?" he drawled at meal hour. "My cabin is spruced up fine as a parlor."

"Yes, it does look nice," replied Mrs. Keetch complacently. "Rebecca has had that in mind to do for some time."

"Wal, it was turrible good of her," said Monty.

"Oh, nonsense," returned Rebecca, with a

swift blush. "Ma wanted you to be more comfortable, that's all."

Monty escaped somehow, as he always managed to escape when catastrophe impended. But one August night when the harvest moon rose white and huge above the black canyon rim he felt such a strange impelling presentiment that he could not bear to leave his porch and go into bed. It had been a hard day—one in which the accumulated cut of alfalfa had been heavy. Canyon Walls Ranch, with its soil and water and sun, was beyond doubt a gold mine. All over southern Utah the ranchers were clamoring for that record alfalfa crop.

The hour was late. The light in Rebecca's room had long been out. Frogs and owls and nighthawks had ceased their lonely calls. Only the insects hummed in the melancholy stillness.

A rustle startled Monty. Was it a leaf falling from a cottonwood? A dark form crossed the barred patches of moonlight. Rebecca! She passed close to him as he lounged on the porch steps. Her face flashed white. She ran down the lane and then stopped to look back.

"Doggone! Am I drunk or crazy or just moonstruck?" said Monty rising. "What is the gurl up to? . . . Shore she seen me heah. . . . Shore she did!"

He started down the lane and when he came out of the shadow of the cottonwoods into the moonlight she began to run with the speed of a deer. Monty stalked after her. He was roused now. He would see this thing through. If this was just another of her hoydenish tricks! But there seemed to be something mysterious in this night flight out into the canyon under the full moon.

Monty lost sight of her at the end of the lane. But when he reached it and turned into the field he saw her on the other side, lingering, looking back. He could see her moonblanched face. She ran on and he followed.

That side of the canyon lay clear in the silver light. On the other the looming canyon wall stood up black, with its level rim moonfired against the sky. The alfalfa shone bright, and the scent of it in the night air was overpowering in its sweetness.

Rebecca was making for the upper end where that day the alfalfa had been cut. She let Monty gain on her, but at last with a burst of laughter she ran to the huge silver-shining haystack and began to climb it.

Monty did not run; he slowed down. He did not know what was happening to him, but his state seemed to verge upon lunacy. One of his nightmares! He would awaken presently. But there was the white form scrambling up the steep haystack. That afternoon he had finished this mound of alfalfa, with the satisfaction of an artist.

When he reached it Rebecca had not only gained the top, but was lying flat, propped on her elbows. Monty went closer—until he was standing right up against the stack. He could see her distinctly now, scarcely fifteen feet above his head. The moonlight lent her form an air of witchery. But it was the mystery of her eyes that completed the bewitchment of Monty. Why had he followed her? He could do nothing. His former threat was but an idle memory. His anger would not rise. She would make him betray his secret and then, alas! Canyon Walls could no longer be a home for him.

"Howdy, Sam," she said, in a tone that he could not comprehend.

"Rebecca, what you doin' out heah?"

"Isn't it a glorious night?"

"Yes. But you ought to be in your bed. An' you could have watched from your window."

"Oh, no. I had to be out in it. . . . Besides, I wanted to make you follow me."

"Wal, you shore have. I was plumb scared, I reckon. An'—an' I'm glad it was only in fun. . . . But why did you want me to follow you?"

"For one thing, I wanted you to see me climb your new haystack."

"Yes? Wal, I've seen you. So come down now. If your mother should ketch us out heah—"

"And I wanted you to see me slide down *this* one."

As he looked up at her he realized how helpless he was in the hands of this strange girl. He kept staring, not knowing what she would do next.

"And *I* wanted to see—terribly—what you'd do," she went on, with a seriousness that surely must have been mockery.

"Rebecca, honey, I don't aim to do—nothin'," replied Monty almost mournfully.

She got to her knees, and leaned over as if to see more clearly. Then she turned round to sit down and slide to the very edge. Her hands were clutched deep in the alfalfa.

"You won't spank me, Sam?" she asked, in impish glee.

"No. Much as I'd like to—an' as you shore need it—I cain't."

"Bluffer . . . Gentile cowpuncher . . . showing yellow . . . marble-hearted fiend!"

"Not thet last, Rebecca. For all my many faults, not that," he said sadly.

She seemed fighting to let go of something that the mound of alfalfa represented only in symbol. Surely the physical effort for Rebecca to hold her balance there could not account for the look of strain on her body and face. And, in addition, all the mystery of Canyon Walls and the beauty of the night hovered over her.

"Sam, dare me to slide," she taunted.

"No," he retorted grimly.

"Coward!"

"Shore. You hit me on the haid there."

Then ensued a short silence. He could see her quivering. She was moving, almost imperceptibly. Her eyes, magnified by the shadow and light, transfixed Monty.

"Gentile, dare me to slide—into your arms," she cried a little quaveringly.

"Mormon tease! Would you—"

"Dare me!"

"Wal, I dare—you, Rebecca . . . but so help me Gawd I won't answer for the consequences."

Her laugh, like the sweet, wild trill of a night bird, rang out, but this time it was full of joy, of certainty, of surrender. And she let go her hold, to spread wide her arms and come sliding on an avalanche of silver hay down upon him.

6

Next morning Monty found work in the fields impossible. He roamed about like a man possessed, and at last went back to the cabin. It was just before the noonday meal. In the ranch house Rebecca hummed a tune while she set the table. Mrs. Keetch sat in her rocker, busy with work on her lap. There was no charged atmosphere. All seemed serene.

Monty responded to the girl's shy glance by taking her hand and leading her up to her mother.

"Ma'am," he began hoarsely, "you've knowed long how my feelin's are for Rebecca. But it seems she—she loves me, too. ... How thet come about I cain't say. It's

145

shore the wonderfullest thing. . . . Now I ask
you—fer Rebecca's sake most—what can be
done about this heah trouble?"

"Daughter, is it true?" asked Mrs. Keetch,
looking up with serene and smiling face.

"Yes, Mother," replied Rebecca simply.

"You love Sam?"

"Oh, I do."

"Since when?"

"Always, I guess. But I never knew till this
June."

"I am very glad, Rebecca," replied the
mother, rising to embrace her. "Since you
could not or would not love one of your own
creed it is well that you love this man who
came a stranger to our gates. He is strong,
he is true, and what his religion is matters
little."

Then she smiled upon Monty. "My son, no
man can say what guided your steps to Canyon Walls. But I always felt God's intent in
it. You and Rebecca shall marry."

"Oh, Mother," murmured the girl raptur-
ously, and she hid her face.

"Wal, I'm willin' an' happy," stammered
Monty. "But I ain't worthy of her, ma'am,
an' you know thet old—"

She silenced him. "You must go to White
Sage and be married at once."

"At once!— When?" faltered Rebecca.

"Aw, Mrs. Keetch, I—I wouldn't hurry the
gurl. Let her have her own time."

"No, why wait? She has been a strange,

starved creature. . . . Tomorrow you must take her to be wed, Sam."

"Wal an' good, if Rebecca says so," said Monty with wistful eagerness.

"Yes," she whispered. "Will you go with us, Ma?"

"Yes," suddenly cried Mrs. Keetch, as if inspired. "I will go. I will cross the Utah line once more before I am carried over. . . . But not White Sage. We will go to Kanab. You shall be married by the bishop."

In the excitement and agitation that possessed mother and daughter at that moment, Monty sensed a significance more than just the tremendous importance of impending marriage. Some deep, strong motive was urging Mrs. Keetch to go to Kanab, there to have the bishop marry Rebecca to a gentile. One way or another it did not matter to Monty. He rode in the clouds. He could not believe in his good luck. Never in his life had he touched such happiness as he was experiencing now.

The womenfolk were an hour late in serving lunch, and during the meal the air of vast excitement permeated their every word and action. They could not have tasted the food on their plates.

"Wal, this heah seems like a Sunday," said Monty, after a hasty meal. "I've loafed a lot this mawnin'. But I reckon I'll go back to work now."

"Oh, Sam—don't—when—when we're

leaving so soon," remonstrated Rebecca shyly.

"When are we leavin'?"

"Tomorrow—early."

"Wal, I'll get thet alfalfa up anyhow. It might rain, you know.—Rebecca, do you reckon you could get up at daylight fer this heah ride?"

"I could stay up all night, Sam."

Mrs. Keetch laughed at them. "There's no rush. We'll start after breakfast, and get to Kanab early enough to make arrangements for the wedding next day. It will give Sam time to buy a respectable suit of clothes to be married in."

"Doggone! I hadn't thought of thet," replied Monty ruefully.

"Sam Hill, you don't marry *me* in a ten-gallon hat, a red shirt and blue overalls, and boots," declared Rebecca.

"How about wearin' my gun?" drawled Monty.

"Your gun!" exclaimed Rebecca.

"Shore. You've forgot how I used to pack it. I might need it there to fight off them Mormons who're so crazy about you."

"Heavens! You leave that gun home."

Next morning when Monty brought the buckboard around, Mrs. Keetch and Rebecca appeared radiant of face, gorgeous of apparel. But for the difference in age anyone might have mistaken the mother for the intended bride.

The drive to Kanab, with fresh horses and light load, took six hours. And the news of the wedding spread over Kanab like wildfire in dry prairie grass. For all Monty's keen eyes he never caught a jealous look, nor did he hear a critical word. That settled with him for all time the status of the Keetchs' Mormon friends. The Tyler brothers came into town and made much of the fact that Monty would soon be one of them. And they planned another fall hunt for wild mustangs and deer. This time Monty would surely bring in Rebecca's wild pony. Waking hours sped by and sleeping hours were few. Almost before Monty knew what was happening he was in the presence of the Mormon bishop.

"Will you come into the Mormon Church?" asked the bishop.

"Wal, sir, I cain't be a Mormon," replied Monty in perplexity. "But I shore have respect fer you people an' your Church. I reckon I never had no religion. I can say I'll never stand in Rebecca's way, in anythin' pertainin' to hers."

"In the event she bears you children you will not seek to raise them gentiles?"

"I'd leave thet to Rebecca," replied Monty quietly.

"And the name Sam Hill, by which you are known, is a middle name?"

"Shore, jist a cowboy middle name."

So they were married. Monty feared they would never escape from the many friends

149

and the curious crowd. But at last they were safely in the buckboard, speeding homeward. Monty sat in the front seat alone. Mrs. Keetch and Rebecca occupied the rear seat. The girl's expression of pure happiness touched Monty and made him swear deep in his throat that he would try to deserve her love. Mrs. Keetch had evidently lived through one of the few great events of her life. What dominated her feelings Monty could not divine, but she had the look of a woman who asked no more of life. Somewhere, at some time, a monstrous injustice or wrong had been done the Widow Keetch. Recalling the bishop's strange look at Rebecca—a look of hunger—Monty pondered deeply.

The ride home, being downhill, with a pleasant breeze off the desert, and that wondrous panorama coloring and spreading in the setting sun, seemed all too short for Monty. He drawled to Rebecca, when they reached the portal of Canyon Walls and halted under the gold-leaved cottonwoods: "Wal, wife, heah we are home. But we shore ought to have made thet honeymoon drive a longer one."

That suppertime was the only one in which Monty ever saw the Widow Keetch bow her head and give thanks to the Lord for the salvation of these young people so strangely brought together, for the home overflowing with milk and honey, for the hopeful future.

* * *

They had their fifth cutting of alfalfa in September, and it was in the nature of an event. The Tyler boys rode over to help, fetching Sue to visit Rebecca. And there was much merrymaking. Rebecca would climb every mound of alfalfa and slide down screaming her delight. And once she said to Monty, "Young man, you should pray under every haystack you build."

"Ahuh. An' what fer should I pray, Rebecca?" he drawled.

"To give thanks for all this sweet-smelling alfalfa has brought you."

The harvest god smiled on Canyon Walls that autumn. Three wagons plied between Kanab and the ranch for weeks, hauling the produce that could not be used. While Monty went off with the Tyler boys for their hunt in Buckskin Forest, the womenfolk and their guests, and the hired hands, applied themselves industriously to the happiest work of the year—preserving all they could of the luscious fruit yield of the season.

Monty came back to a home such as had never been his even in his happiest dreams. Rebecca was incalculably changed, and so happy that Monty trembled as he listened to her sing, as he watched her at work. The mystery never ended for him, not even when she whispered that they might expect a little visitor from the angels next spring. But Monty's last doubt faded, and he gave himself over to work, to his loving young wife, to walks in the dusk under the canyon walls, to a lonely pipe beside his little fireside.

The winter passed, and spring came, doubling all former activities. They had taken over the canyon three miles to the westward, which once cleared of brush and cactus and rock promised well. The problem had been water and Monty solved it by extending a new irrigation ditch from the same brook that watered the home ranch. Good fortune had attended his every venture.

Around the middle of April, when the cottonwoods began to be tinged with green and the peach trees with pink, Monty began to grow restless about the coming event. It uplifted him one moment, appalled him the next. In that past which seemed so remote to him now, he had snuffed out life. Young, fiery, grim Smoke Bellew! And by some incomprehensible working out of life he was now about to bring life into being.

On the seventeenth of May, some hours after breakfast, he was hurriedly summoned from the fields. His heart appeared to be choking him.

Mrs. Keetch met him at the porch. He scarcely knew her.

"My son, do you remember this date?"

"No," replied Monty wonderingly.

"Two years ago today you came to us. . . . And Rebecca has just borne you a son."

"Aw—my Gawd!— How—how is she, ma'am?" he gasped.

"Both well. We could ask no more. It has all been a visitation of God. . . . Come."

Some days later the important matter of christening the youngster came up.

"Ma wants one of those jaw-breaking Biblical names," said Rebecca pouting. "But I like just plain Sam."

"Wal, it ain't much of a handle fer sech a wonderful little feller."

"It's your name. I love it."

"Rebecca, you kinda forget Sam Hill was jist a—a sort of a middle name. It ain't my real name."

"Oh, yes, I remember now," replied Rebecca, her great eyes lighting. "At Kanab—the bishop asked about Sam Hill. Mother had told him that was your nickname."

"Darlin', I had another nickname once," he said sadly.

"So, my man with a mysterious past. And what was that?"

"They called me Smoke."

"How funny! . . . Well, I may be Mrs. Monty Smoke Bellew, according to the law and the Church, but *you*, my husband, will always be Sam Hill to me!"

"An' the boy?" asked Monty enraptured.

"Is Sam Hill, too."

An anxious week passed and then all seemed surely well with the new mother and baby. Monty ceased to tiptoe around. He no longer awoke with a start in the dead of night.

Then one Saturday as he came out on the wide porch, he heard a hallo from someone, and saw four riders coming through the portal. A bolt shot back from a closed door of his memory. Arizona riders! How well he knew the lean faces, the lithe forms, the gun belts, the mettlesome horses!

"Nix, fellers," called the foremost rider, as Monty came slowly out.

An instinct followed by a muscular contraction that had the speed of lightning passed over Monty. Then he realized he packed no gun and was glad. Old habit might have been too strong. His hawk eye saw lean hands drop from hips. A sickening feeling of despair followed his first reaction.

"Howdy, Smoke," drawled the foremost rider.

"Wal, doggone! If it ain't Jim Sneed," returned Monty, as he recognized the sheriff, and he descended the steps to walk out and offer his hand, quick to see the swift, penetrating eyes run over him.

"Shore, it's Jim. I reckoned you'd know me. Hoped you would, as I wasn't too keen about raisin' your smoke."

"Ahuh. What you all doin' over heah, Jim?" asked Monty, with a glance at the three watchful riders.

"Main thing I come over fer was to buy

stock fer Strickland. An' he said if it wasn't out of my way I might fetch you back. Word come thet you'd been seen in Kanab. An' when I made inquiry at White Sage I shore knowed who Sam Hill was."

"I see. Kinda tough it happened to be Strickland. Doggone! My luck jist couldn't last."

"Smoke, you look uncommon fine," said the sheriff with another appraising glance. "You shore haven't been drinkin'. An' I seen fust off you wasn't totin' no gun."

"Thet's all past fer me, Jim."

"Wal, I'll be damned!" exclaimed Sneed, and fumbled for a cigarette. "Bellew, I jist don't savvy."

"Reckon you wouldn't. . . . Jim, I'd like to ask if my name ever got linked up with thet Green Valley deal two years an' more ago?"

"No, it didn't, Smoke, I'm glad to say. Your pards Slim an' Cuppy pulled thet. Slim was killed coverin' Cuppy's escape."

"Ahuh . . . So Slim—wal, wal—" sighed Monty, and paused a moment to gaze into space.

"Smoke, tell me your deal heah," said Sneed.

"Shore. But would you mind comin' indoors?"

"Reckon I wouldn't. But Smoke, I'm still figgerin' you the cowboy."

"Wal, you're way off. Get down an' come in."

Monty led the sheriff into Rebecca's bedroom. She was awake, playing with the baby by her side on the bed.

"Jim, this is my wife an' youngster," said Monty feelingly. "An' Rebecca, this heah is an old friend of mine, Jim Sneed, from Arizona."

That must have been a hard moment for the sheriff—the cordial welcome of the blushing wife, the smiling mite of a baby who was clinging to his finger, the atmosphere of unadulterated joy in the little home.

At any rate, when they went out again to the porch Sneed wiped his perspiring face and swore at Monty, "—— cowboy, have you gone an' double-crossed thet sweet gurl?"

Monty told him the few salient facts of his romance, and told it with trembling eagerness to be believed.

"So you've turned Mormon?" said the sheriff.

"No, but I'll be true to these women. . . . An' one thing I ask, Sneed. Don't let it be known in White Sage or heah *why* I'm with you. . . . I can send word to my wife I've got to go to Arizona . . . then afterward I'll come back."

"Smoke, I wish I had a stiff drink," replied Sneed. "But I reckon you haven't anythin'?"

"Only water an' milk."

"Good Lawd! For an Arizonian!" Sneed halted at the head of the porch steps and shot out a big hand. His cold eyes had warmed.

"Smoke, may I tell Strickland you'll send him some money now an' then—till thet debt is paid?"

Monty stared and faltered, "Jim—you shore can."

"Fine," returned the sheriff in a loud voice, and he strode down the steps to mount his horse. "Adios, cowboy. Be good to thet little woman."

Monty could not speak. He watched the riders down the lane, out into the road, and through the wide canyon gates to the desert beyond. His heart was full. He thought of Slim and Cuppy, those young firebrand comrades of his range days. He could remember now without terror. He could live once more with his phantoms of the past. He could see lean, lithe Arizona riders come into Canyon Walls, if that event ever chanced again, and be glad of their coming.

FROM THE ASHES

Volume Two in the
Bon Marché Chronicles

by

CHET HAGAN

Available wherever fine books are sold

September 1, 1990

An Introduction to
From the Ashes
by Chet Hagan

In *Bon Marché,* acclaimed historical novelist Chet Hagan introduced readers to the remarkable Dewey dynasty, a family of emigrants from Europe who fought to make a place for themselves on the American frontier. Swept up in the turbulent history of a growing nation, the Dewey family found fortune in the rough river town of Nashville, Tennessee. There, the clan's founder realized his greatest dream: to build a great estate dedicated to the breeding and racing of fine horses—Bon Marché.

From the Ashes, the second epic volume in the Bon Marché Chronicles, begins in 1846. Nashville is becoming a bustling commercial center, and Bon Marché has developed into one of America's most important stud farms.

In the aftermath of the death of Charles Dewey, the management of the plantation passes into the iron hand of his daughter Alma May, known as "The Princess." She continues the Dewey tradition through her shrewd management and uncompromising business sense. And she scandalizes the gossip-mongers of Nashville, who watch her affairs being conducted in the open without regard for public opinion.

But the fortunes of Bon Marché are threatened by the ominous rumblings of the War Between the States. As the issue of slavery tears apart the family, Alma May's ruthless ambition causes the family fortune to grow, leading to new farms in Kentucky and Long Island, New York, and investments in a newspaper empire. Her son, Charles II, sets out on a trek west to California to begin a new Dewey enterprise, and the younger members of the Dewey family must rebuild their lives from the ashes of a devastating war.

An American saga in the grandest tradition, with a scope as broad as the country it portrays, *From the Ashes* is an epic novel—filled with grand passion, abiding love, and unbridled courage—by a major new name in historical fiction.

Prologue

Charles Dewey was dead.

The master of Nashville's Bon Marché stud had gone to meet his Maker and there were those among Dewey's friends who wondered how God would contend with him.

"The Lord will be glad to consign him to the Devil," one of his fellow horsemen suggested with only partial humor, "when He learns Charles intends to manage Heaven."

*Green grow the laurel, all sparkling with dew,
I'm lonely, my darling, since parting from
 you . . .*

Brevet Captain Albert Dewey, late of West
Point, was disquieted and morose. Worse—
he had begun to doubt his own worth, a new
and alien thought for a young man who had
been taught, almost from birth, that he had
a gift from God to be someone special. That
to be a *Dewey* was the best possible circum-
stance in the human experience.

*But by the next morning I hope to prove true,
And change the green laurel for the red,
 white, and blue.*

The poignant song, accompanied by the
mournful wail of a mountain man's fiddle,
drifted up to him from the campfires of the
American army ringing Matamoros, Mexico.
It added to his discomfort. Had he "proved
true" in this first test under fire in this
strange war? He was uncertain. But of one
thing he was sure: the glory of battle, as
preached in the classrooms at the United

States Military Academy, was a lie. His instructors had engaged in sophistry, filling his brain with their subtle arguments about the grandeur of military engagement. It had been deceit, nothing but deceit.

Oh, God, how naive I've been!

Instead of being grand, the warfare he had seen thus far had been ill-planned, totally confused, and largely commanded by incompetents. His despondency told him he was one of those—a rank incompetent.

There had been no war when he came to what was known as Fort Texas, a hurriedly constructed, star-shaped earthworks redoubt on the Rio Grande River opposite the city of Matamoros. No war and, indeed, little thought there would be war. Mexico had been enraged by the admission of an independent Texas as the twenty-eighth state in the American Union. But no one in real authority in the army commanded by "Old Rough and Ready" Zachary Taylor believed there would be war. Mexican anger, everyone contended, would not, could not, be translated into fighting, given the disorganized nature of the Mexican government. Everyone said a show of American strength on the Rio Grande would be enough to deter the Mexicans.

"Everyone" had been wrong!

A Mexican army (under the command of General Mariano Arista, they would learn later) struck across the Rio Grande late in

April of 1846 with a large force of cavalry, butchering an American patrol of sixty-three men. With such ease, it seemed. And then there had been fighting at a place called Palo Alto, little more than a meadow of tall, dusty saw grass; also on the low banks of a dry streambed the official reports would designate as Resaca de la Palma.

Brevet Captain Dewey's command was a hastily organized company of the volunteers who were pouring into Texas. His temporary promotion had come because he was a West Pointer and, as such, was expected to have the training necessary for the task of molding the "vols" into a fighting force. They were rabble. An unsavory bunch: adventurers, petty criminals, brawlers—almost all unwilling to accept discipline.

Nevertheless, he had tried.

He remembered it now as a series of searing vignettes not mentioned in his diary, because he found it emotionally impossible to put it into written words. But the memories remained and he could not erase them.

The May morning at Resaca de la Palma had been beautiful, the golden sunshine gleaming off the massed bayonets of his company. The exquisite fragrance of prairie wildflowers wafted along on gentle winds. His men stood before him, their lack of military unity reflected in the ragged ranks: some at attention, some at ease, some with partial uniforms, some with no uniforms at all. Yet, there was something mesmerizing about the moment. Maybe it was the beauty of the day. Maybe it was the company guidons snapping smartly in the breeze. Maybe it was Dewey's West Point orientation on the glory of battle.

Whatever it was, the captain felt the necessity to address his command. He sat ramrod straight on the back of his horse.

"Men!" he had shouted. "I am not going to ask you to be brave on this day, because to do so would only insult you. Only brave men would be standing there now in your ranks, ready to defend our flag—to safeguard the honor of our country!"

Huzzahs rose up from the infantrymen.

"But bravery does not require that you be foolhardy. Be calm. Be resolute. Keep in mind, men, when the roar of battle is upon you, that only a small proportion of the shots fired in combat are effective." Captain Dewey had even laughed at that point. "An old drill sergeant once told me that men shoot dreadful careless in battle—"

There were guffaws in the ranks.

"—But be not careless yourselves. Be sure of your shots. Make them count. And a benevolent God will see you through—to victory!"

"TO VICTORY!" the volunteers had bellowed in response.

In truth, there *had* been victory that day at Resaca de la Palma. But at what cost?

The benevolent God of whom the captain had spoken was represented on the other side as well. They had not faced a heathen horde; it had been a clash of two Christian armies, both worshiping the same Supreme Being. Had He looked away? Had He abandoned them both, in His disgust at what they were doing, to the forces of Hell? Albert Dewey believed so now, unable to drive from his mind the stark realities of what he had witnessed.

The enemy had been massed across a chaparral, raking it with grapeshot and musket fire, as Dewey's company led a flanking attack. A private—Dewey didn't know his name, but he was just a beardless lad—had been running alongside the captain's horse, screaming defiance at the Mexicans. Suddenly, his headlong dash was stopped by the impact of a musket ball full in the face, frozen for an instant in death before he fell. His blood had spattered Albert's boot.

And there was Sergeant William Gordon, who had been leading his squad in a charge on a cannon emplacement in the center of the Mexican line. They were only a scant ten yards from their goal when the cannon fired once more, the heavy ball striking the sergeant in the left leg, severing it at the knee, sending the limb flying grotesquely through the air. Before the fieldpiece could be reloaded, Gordon's squad overwhelmed the position, bayoneting the Mexican gunners, breaching the line. Captain Dewey had written a report to General Taylor recommending Sergeant Gordon be decorated as a hero. Posthumously.

When the Mexican line broke and a general rout was under way—the enemy throwing away weapons, dropping cartridge boxes, stripping off uniforms as if somehow making themselves lighter so they might run faster—Lieutenant George Seimanski, waving his sword cavalierly, exhorted his men to give chase. He tripped inadvertently, sprawling facedown on the turf. In the blink of an eye, a retreating Mexican lancer wheeled his horse, plunging his lance through his foe's back, pinioning him to the ground. One of the company's backwoods riflemen shot the lancer off his mount. Too late. The young officer's lifeblood nourished the wildflowers.

The Resaca de la Palma victory was bought in that manner. Two days later, the United States formally declared war, President James K. Polk saying in Washington: "The cup of forbearance has been exhausted." Still, more than a week went by before General Taylor chanced ordering his army across the Rio Grande to invest the city of Matamoros, as the regimental band gaily played "Yankee Doodle." General Arista had long since withdrawn his forces from the area; the opportunity to destroy them had been lost by the American delay.

In one sense, encampment at Matamoros

was even worse for Brevet Captain Dewey than the battle. At least under battle conditions his disreputable, ill-trained volunteers were free to do what they did best—fight and kill. They adapted poorly to the idleness of camp life. Regular drills were impossible; desertions were commonplace.

Dewey sat now in his field tent, trying to compose a letter to the mother of a dead regular soldier from Mississippi, one of the very few regulars in his company. Details of his death sickened Albert. On the night before, a whiskey-crazed volunteer had raped a Mexican woman in a house in Matamoros, stabbing the screaming woman to death in full view of her three terrified children. In the row that followed, Corporal Vernon Mayfield had tried to arrest the offender, who pulled a pistol and shot him dead, fleeing the scene. He was still at large and would probably never be caught.

Albert had written the date—"Wednesday, May 20, 1846"—and the salutation: "My dear Mrs. Mayfield . . ."

He had wrestled with his conscience before committing the first sentence to the paper: "I regret to inform you that your son, Corporal Vernon Mayfield, has given his life in the service of his nation."

Dewey groaned. As a company commander there would be more such letters to be done, inane and devoid of the detail that might reveal to the survivors the senseless nature of their losses. How many other lies would he have to tell?

The canvas flap of his tent parted, his Negro orderly entering, saluting smartly. The captain returned the salute lazily.

"A letter fer ya, suh."

"Thank you, Cephus." Reaching for it, his heart jumped; the address was in Virginia's hand. Dewey tore it open quickly, ignoring the orderly's departing salute:

My darling Albert,
We all miss you terribly, but no more desperately than today, because Bon Marché has suffered a cruel blow. I wish for some way to spare you this news, but I'm not clever enough to sugar-coat the reality of what I must tell you. Sometime during last night [the letter was dated Friday, June 12—more than a month earlier] your grandmother was stricken. The doctor tells us she has suffered a stroke and he says her condition threatens her life.

The captain cursed under his breath.

She has lost the use of her limbs on the right side; also the power to speak properly. But, on a more positive note, Dr. Thompson assures us her heart is strong and that there are many examples of sufficient recovery from strokes so that the victim can resume a long and productive life. Providence controls that, he says, and it is for that we all pray now, knowing your prayers will join our own.

Wanting to get this into the post immediately, I will add only that all of the children are well. Until that happy day when you shall return to them, and to me, I send my undying love.

Your adoring Virginia.

Albert kissed the letter. That had become a ritual for him. Kissing her letters, which she had touched, allowed him to imagine touching her, kissing her.

Then, he wept. Not so much because of the critical illness of his step-grandmother, but because of his frustrations. More than anything in life he wanted to be part of Bon Marché at that moment. The realization surprised him. When he was growing up there he had no ambitions to follow in his late father's footsteps as the Bon Marché breeding manager. Perhaps he had been too close to the plantation to fully appreciate it. He tried to remember why it was he had appealed to his grandfather, the founder of Bon Marché, to use his influence to secure an appointment to the United States Military Academy. His choice of a soldier's life, he mused, had been a terrible mistake, and not one easily corrected.

Green grow the laurel, all sparkling with dew,
I'm lonely, my darling, since parting from
you . . .

Virginia's lovely face appeared before him,
framed by ringlets of blond curls, just as he
had seen her on their wedding day at Bon
Marché. It had been more than a year since
he had *really* seen her, when he handed her
into a carriage at Fort Jesup, Louisiana, and
watched her being carried away toward
Nashville, their fourth child still nestled in
her womb.

Would he ever see his new son, Staunch?
Would he ever see any of his children again?
Jeff and Jack, such proper little gentlemen.
And sweet Carolina, a perfect copy of her
mother. She had started to walk since they
had parted, another important moment his
military service had cost him.

Singers in the camp began again: "Green
grow the laurel, all sparkling . . ."

"Damned song!" Dewey muttered audibly.
"Don't they know anything else?"

It was a ballad so pervasive among the
men of the American army that Mexican
tongues, trying to sing it in derision, had cor-
rupted the first two words, "green grow,"
into "gringo," a hard, double-syllable im-
agery of the invaders. *Gringo!* It had become
a bitter malediction.

I'm lonely, my darling, since parting . . .

x

The captain left his field desk and his odious writing chores, tossing himself onto a cot in his despair, staring up at the canvas ceiling, permitting his thoughts to transport him to Bon Marché.

II

As the chestnut filly, Mattie's Darling, swept across the finish line, four easy lengths the better in the second and decisive heat of the match race, the Frenchman raised his glass to George Washington Dewey.

"I salute you, monsieur—the premier trainer at Metairie!"

Dewey acknowledged the compliment with a sober nod. "Thank you, Bernard." There was none of the exuberance one might have expected from a winner.

"If I continue to follow your horses, George," the Frenchman laughed, "I may yet recoup the family fortune before the meeting is ended."

"Let's hope you do." The trainer got to his feet. "You'll excuse us, Bernard . . . we have a dinner engagement." He reached out a hand to his wife.

Making their way to their carriage through the departing crowd at the Metairie Racecourse, they were stopped frequently by others offering congratulations on the filly's victory. Dewey was strangely annoyed by it all, and showed it. He was a stockily built man, with graying, thinning hair, his square-cut face capable of a terrible scowl, which was what he put forth as he pushed through the throng.

Once in the carriage, instantly put into motion by the top-hatted Negro driver, his wife chided him sharply: "Georgie, sometimes you can be quite rude."

"I just didn't feel like indulging the sycophants today."

"Sycophants? Certainly you can't put Monsieur de Mandeville in that class, and you were rude to him, too. That was a rather clumsy white lie about a dinner engagement."

Dewey laughed sarcastically. "The truth, my dear, of what I feel about the vaunted Bernard Xavier de Marigny de Mandeville would have been a good deal more clumsy, believe me. The man is an ass."

"Georgie!"

"And for God's sake, Mary, stop calling me 'Georgie.' "

She pouted. "You used to love it."

"Maybe I did. But I've grown up since then. In the event you're not aware of it, I'm fifty-six years old." There was an iniquitous grin. "Meaning that you, Mrs. Dewey, must be fifty-eight."

"Georgie! It's absolutely horrid for you to remind me."

The husband groaned.

Mary Dewey fell into a sullen silence as they drove through the bustling, humid city of New Orleans. A plumpish matron, she had been a beauty as a young woman; only vestiges remained. There was some compensation for lost beauty in the expensively stylish gowns she wore, and the lavish cosmetic attention she paid to her face. Still, she hadn't considered age a foe until recent months when George seemed to lose interest in her. That coincided with his first objection to the loving appellation of "Georgie." She had seen such erosion in other marriages, but never imagined it would happen in her own.

The carriage entered Chartres Street where the Deweys maintained a three-story brick town house. It stood as a reminder of another argument they had had, when Mary had insisted on the purchase of the property because it was in the center of the social life of the city. She understood that George might have been more comfortable remaining in the country, some ten miles north of New Orleans, at Nouveau Marché, the stud farm he patterned after his father's in Tennessee. But she reasoned he was working too hard there and it was time for George Junior, at twenty-four, to assume a management role in the family's breeding and racing enterprises.

Dewey, never able to deny his wife what she really wanted, had acquiesced in the matter of the fashionable town house. After that the elder George's life had become a series of daily carriage rides from Chartres Street to the Metairie track and back again, being involved with his horses only enough to be given unwarranted credit for their successes.

This day had been an example of that. It was George Junior who bred the filly they named Mattie's Darling, who broke her, and who brought her up to racing condition. The father had merely saddled her for the match, a ceremonial chore at best, and had accepted the accolades of his peers for having brought her to victory. It was an empty thing for him. His thoughts took him back to his days at Bon Marché in Nashville, when he had trained the dam of Mattie's Darling, a tough, hard-knocking competitor named Matilda in honor of his stepmother. Matilda, bred by his late father, carried the blood of the great Messenger.

Dewey recognized he was fortunate in having a son who would sublimate his own ego for the good of the family business. That both pleased and appalled him. He never would have been capable of such easy sublimation and he wasn't certain he welcomed it in a young man carrying not only his blood but his name. Somehow, he saw it as a weakness in Junior.

At that moment George Washington Dewey Sr. was sure of only one thing: his utter boredom. Bored with what racing had become for him, bored with Mary's constant social posturing, bored with the opera, with the theater, with the masked balls, with intimate dinners for effete Frenchmen claiming ancient titles and Spanish planters prattling about their wealth, with the incessant gossip about quadroons (who had tinges of Negro blood, as if it really mattered), and bored, too, with the ever-present quaintness of New Orleans. To him it would always be a suspect city; a foreign place, American only by the accident of geography.

When they entered the town house, George went at once to the drawing room, where he poured himself a liberal portion of bourbon. Downing it in one gulp, he sank into an easy chair, sighed deeply, and put back his head, closing his eyes.

Mary studied him for a moment or two. Then: "George, what *is* it?"

"I'm weary is all."

"It's Two, isn't it?"

The eyes opened. "What about him?"

"Georgie, sometimes you can be so damned exasperating!"

Dewey sighed once more. "I thought we agreed we weren't going to hash over ... well, the saga of Charles Dewey the Second again. Wasn't that our last word on it?"

"Yes, but—" She sat down opposite him. "I wish you'd make peace with Two. He's corrected his error, you know, by marrying the girl. And their son, after all, is our grand-child."

"He brought dishonor to the Dewey name."

"There are times when you can be such a hypocrite."

"So we're back to that again," he said bitterly.

"Yes, we are, because I can remember when he was sowing his wild oats how you used to laugh about it. 'A chip off the old block,' you'd say proudly."

"That was no excuse for him to be stupid about it."

Mary tried to keep anger from her voice. "It was you who always taught the children to be self-sufficient, to make their own choices in life. In sum, that was Two's only sin."

George smiled wanly, seeing a way to possibly redirect the conversation away from the subject of his eldest son. "I did, didn't I? Well, Mary, it seems to have worked out well for everyone but the man who gave the advice."

"What does that mean?"

"I'm talking about all this"—he made an all-encompassing gesture with his arms— "this artificial life we lead . . . this unrewarding mess—" He got to his feet, making for the bourbon bottle again. "Mary, I feel a lack of *reason* for my life."

"Georgie! You're frightening me."

He poured a drink, looking up at his image in the large, gilt-framed mirror over the mantel, not liking what he saw. An aging man stood before him, filled with doubts.

"When we were growing up at Bon Marché," he tried to explain, "my father put a challenge in our way every single day of the year. And we were expected to meet those challenges. I don't have that any longer."

There was a silence; she unsure of what to say, he caught up in his melancholy.

Suddenly, Dewey turned back to his wife, a decision made. "I'll be catching the packet boat for Nashville in the morning."

Mary gasped. "Why?"

"I'm going back to Bon Marché to claim my inheritance."

"Your inheritance!"

"That's right. I was there at the beginning when Charles Dewey started Bon Marché. I played a role in building that estate—a major role, no one can deny. Now, from everything we are told in the letters, Mattie may be nearing the end of her days. It's time for me to take over, to assume my responsibilities."

"You're mad!"

"No, Mary, I've just come to my senses. Bon Marché is where I belong."

"New Orleans is where you belong," Mary said angrily. "Our roots are *here* now. My God, George, we've been here for more than a decade—"

He cut her off. "Three quarters of my life has been invested in Bon Marché."

"And have you forgotten why we came to New Orleans in the first place? How you were shunted aside at Bon Marché when your stepmother brought in those two cousins of hers to manage the estate? And how your father never lifted a hand to keep you there?"

"I made a mistake in not fighting then," George answered flatly. "I intend to rectify it."

"And destroy what you've built here? You have your own wealth now, your own farm, your own horses. Largely through your efforts the Metairie track was built and—"

"I can sell my Metairie shares to that Ten Broeck fellow. He's been making noises about wanting to control it."

"And Nouveau Marché?"

"Junior is already managing it, isn't he? He can have it all when I take over Bon Marché."

"And what about me, Georgie?" She seemed ready to cry. "Do you have a convenient way to dispose of me, too?"

"I'd hope you'd be with me at Bon Marché."

"And if not?"

"If not," he replied coldly, "you shall have this town house." As an afterthought: "And enough money to maintain yourself, of course."

Mary sank deep into her chair, weeping now. George stood away from her, watching her, making no effort to console her. Nor to further convince her of the rightness of his position. He had made his decision; she'd have to make her own.

It took her several minutes to bring her emotions under control. When she had, she rose and went to George's desk, where she rummaged through some papers before finding what she was seeking.

"Georgie, I've listened to you over the years," she said with determination, "extolling the virtues of New Orleans as a racing center. And I remember it was just a few weeks ago when you read me this—with great pride, as I recall it."

Mary searched through a copy of *American Turf Register and Sporting Magazine.*

"Here it is: 'The horses which run at New Orleans comprise the cracks of several states; the studs of Alabama, Tennessee, Mississippi, and not infrequently the Old Dominion, are annually represented there by their best and bravest.' Isn't that true any longer?"

"It's true."

"Then *why*, as one of the most prominent horsemen in New Orleans, would you want to leave here?"

"As the eldest surviving son of Charles Dewey I have my rights at Bon Marché."

"Your rights!" She laughed derisively. "You can't honestly believe Mattie Dewey is going to abandon her cousins after all those years they've been in charge of that plantation."

"That's exactly why I must press my claims now, *before* my stepmother dies."

Mary shuddered. "I want no part of Nashville."

"Well—" He shrugged. "I can only say I mean to have Bon Marché."

III

Black, scudding clouds maneuvered in the skies over Bon Marché like a fleet of ebony-sailed men-of-war, attacking the more than thirty-five hundred acres of the plantation with torrents of rain. For a moment there was an artificial night in the middle of the late June afternoon, and then broadsides of lightning made the night into instant day as the cannonade of thunder tumbled waves of crashing sounds one over the other.

A small carriage, its driver-passenger sitting open to the sudden storm, sped along the wide road leading to the Bon Marché main house, racing between white-fenced pastures now empty of the thoroughbreds for which the Tennessee farm was renowned. They had been removed to the safety of the big barns. The driver reached out, flicking a whip on the flanks of his lath-

ered horse. Sweeping into the circular drive-
way fronting the mansion, the carriage came
to a sudden stop. A young man, carrying a
black bag, leaped out, taking the steps two
at a time to the veranda. Before he could
knock on the oaken double door, it was
opened by a Negro servant.

"Bad day fer drivin' in an open rig, Dr.
Thompson."

"It is, indeed, Joseph," the visitor agreed
as he entered the house. "The drive from
Nashville turned into an adventure. There
are trees down on the road all along the
way."

The black man nodded, reaching for the
doctor's soaked cape and dripping, broad-
brimmed hat.

"Have someone take care of the horse, will
you? I'm afraid I used him up."

"Yassuh."

Dr. Thompson looked down at his trousers
clinging wetly to his legs. Grasping each knee
of cloth, he flipped the trouser legs back and
forth, sending little sprays of water across
the polished entrance-hall floor.

"They's all waitin' fer ya in Miss Mattie's
bedroom," the servant prodded him, not suc-
cessfully hiding his dismay at the mess the
doctor was making on the floor, a mess he'd
have to mop up.

"Of course." He moved quickly across the
foyer, mounting the curved stairway to the
second floor. It was the third time that week

he had been at Bon Marché. He feared now it would be his last. *Even the Deweys,* he thought, *are not immortal.*

Pushing open the bedroom door, the physician wasn't surprised to find the entire Dewey family in attendance around the bed of Matilda Jackson Dewey, all sober-faced, several of them weeping. It annoyed him somewhat that every time he came to Bon Marché he had to do his doctoring under the stern gazes of the assembled Deweys. Old Dr. Almond, whose own ill health had made it impossible for him to continue to minister to the family, had warned Thompson it would be that way, but the younger man was still uncomfortable with the situation.

"I came as quickly as I could," he explained quietly.

No one in the room spoke as they made way for him to get to the bed, where the daughter, Alma May, sat holding her mother's hand.

The doctor acknowledged her. "Miss Alma," he said as he took the hand from her to feel for a pulse in the wrist. Harry Thompson didn't understand why, but every time he was close to Alma May Dewey illicit thoughts about her coursed through his mind. He wondered whether other men experienced the same phenomenon.

Mattie Dewey's pulse was very weak, its tempo erratic.

"May I have a little hot water in a cup, please?" the doctor requested.

Alma May gestured to one of the black servant girls in the room and within seconds the cup of water was produced. The Deweys were used to such response. A gesture, a snap of the fingers, a meaningful nod of the head, were all commands they expected to be obeyed. Not just by their slaves. The family members were powerful people, at ease with leadership, accustomed to having their own way in all matters.

Reaching into his bag of medicines, Dr. Thompson brought out a bottle of dark-colored liquid, pouring a small portion of it into the water. He swirled the water around in the cup, mixing the medicine with it. It was nothing more than a tonic, a hoped-for mild stimulant for the languid heart; it wouldn't do any real good, but he had to administer something to the dying matriarch of Bon Marché.

"Miss Mattie," he said softly, lifting the patient's head from the pillow, "let's see if we can take a sip or two of this."

Mattie's eyes opened. There was a dull, unseeing vacancy in them.

He put the cup to her lips, tilting it so that a few drops ran into her mouth. She didn't swallow. Perhaps she could no longer swallow, or perhaps she couldn't comprehend she was supposed to swallow. The tonic dribbled out of her mouth and down her chin. Dr.

Thompson mopped at it with his handkerchief, then lowered her head to the pillow once more.

The eyes remained open, staring. The young man closed the lids with a sure, gentle motion.

Conscious of his role as a surrogate for Dr. Almond, Thompson reported, "In our consultations, Dr. Almond and I have discussed the very real possibility that Mrs. Dewey might suffer another seizure. After one paroxysm, it's not unusual another will follow." He sighed. "That, I'm afraid, has happened. In lesser degree, of course, but—"

He looked around at the array of sad faces.

"She's very weak. Quite honestly, there is little more I . . . uh . . . we can do."

"How . . . long?" Alma May asked hesitantly.

"I can't be certain. Hours, perhaps. Yes, no more than a few hours."

Don't miss all the power and majesty of the Bon Marché Chronicles by Chet Hagan, available wherever paperbacks are sold